Belief in the Realm

Books by Starr Green:

•

CASTAWAY STRANGERS

•

Wave Sweeper Trilogy
SAILING IN THE SKY
BELIEF IN THE REALM
TREASURE IN THE DEEP *(Coming Soon)*

•

Praise for the Wave Sweeper Trilogy

"…pairs an autistic teen protagonist with a whimsical plot that makes for a stunning urban-fantasy debut." —**IndieReader**

…light and refreshing read… very sweet story that let's you escape from reality and come out feeling good." —**Rachel Reads**

"…really fast paced and easy to get into… amazing Autism representation…" —**They.Them.Reads**

BELIEF IN THE REALM

Written by

Starr Green

Earthy Info
Portland, Oregon

Copyright © 2022 by Starr Green

This is a work of fiction. Names, characters, places, and incidents either are the product of the author's imagination or are used fictitiously. Any resemblance to actual persons, living or dead, events, or locales is entirely coincidental.

All rights reserved. No part of this book may be reproduced or used in any manner without written permission of the copyright owner except for the use of quotations in a book review.

First edition August 2022
Map design: Megan Scott
Cover design by: Earthy Info
Interior book design by: Earthy Info

ISBN 978-1-955561-13-6 (hardcover)
ISBN 978-1-955561-14-3 (softcover)
ISBN 978-1-955561-15-0 (ebook)

Library of Congress Control Number: 2022944217

Earthy Info
Portland, Oregon
www.earthyinfo.wordpress.com

Pronunciation Guide

Fia — Fee-uh
Lugh — Loo
Manannán Mac Lir — Mon-ah-non Mac Leer
Sidhe Realm — She re-lm
Tua De Dannan — Two-ah Day Dan-on
Tua De (shortened) — Two-ah Day

CHAPTER 1

Piper

Piper tugged at the heavy tangled blankets on the giant canopy bed in a halfhearted attempt at tidying up. Her motions caused a silvery-colored kitten to jump a foot in the air, dislodged from a cozy spot near the footboard.

Unlike most kittens, it didn't land on its feet. Instead, she hovered for a moment using delicate furry wings. "Take care. I was sleeping," Flutter complained, stretching out its front legs with a yawn. The kitten's words dripped into Piper's mind, a recent ability compared to her eighteen years of life holding one-sided conversations with animals.

"You know, I used to talk to myself a lot, but now I have you to talk to," she told Flutter.

"Lucky me." The cat rolled onto its back and went limp, closing her eyes.

Piper padded across the polished wooden floor of the ship's cabin she lived in with the peter-pan-like boy who had built all of this and lived here with her. The youthful god of the sea, or MacLir to anyone who knew him well, looked no older than she did since he was kept from growing older by the sea, but he used his time learning many skills. He'd built the bed, the wardrobe, even the whole ship and named it Wave Sweeper. More recently, he'd put in a modern kitchen along one wall. She smiled, remembering the moment less than a year ago when she'd seen it for the first time. The same day she'd become immortal, like MacLir.

She twisted her honey-brown hair into a simple side braid, while reviewing her clothing options hanging in the massive wardrobe. Choosing what to wear in the morning had always been easy since she owned one pair of jeans and eight of the same blue tee shirt. However, these days one more item of clothing beckoned to her. She ran a hand over the soft, but gorgeous blue dress hanging in the wardrobe. Created for her by pixies and magic, it was her official goddess dress.

She could do magic without the dress on, so she mostly wore her usual clothes, but maybe that would change one day. Perhaps when she was more comfortable with her new powers, she'd consider wearing it all the time.

It still seemed odd she was a Goddess of Love. Having lived an uneventful and sheltered life as an autistic human child until last year. She was still adjusting to both being an adult and living among gods and faeries. A life she could not have guessed was even possible.

Piper also never imagined she'd get struck with baby fever. Not having spent time around children, she didn't know how enchanting they could be. Now she desperately wanted one. Her bedroom door opened into a second, much smaller bedroom, and she paused in the doorway. The room would be perfect for her child.

The empty bed, with its green bedspread and green emeralds embedded in the ceiling, would hold her child one day. Her and MacLir's baby. No matter what people said to her about the impossibility of an elemental having a child, or how it was unheard of for the maiden aspect of love to get pregnant… she'd figure it out. That was a promise she'd made to herself and would not budge. Besides, she enjoyed challenging puzzles to solve.

Determination renewed, she made her way through the empty room and out of the ship's cabin, but the bright sunlight overwhelmed her. Catching her foot on the door jam, she shouted, "Oh, coconuts!" She could sense this would be one of her more painful falls, but was caught by the boy she loved.

He swept her into his arms and cradled her, smiling at her use of his often spoken phrase, and asked, "You okay?"

His almond-shaped turquoise blue eyes sparkled with merriment. They were naturally squinty, especially when smiling, which he did most of the time. His sandy blond hair, spiked from saltwater, topped his soft beardless face with slight dimples.

She was about to say something flirty or suggest they head back to the bed she'd failed to tidy properly, but she caught sight of a man sitting on the L-shaped bench attached to the ship's mast. "Put me down," she said instead.

MacLir shrugged and set her upright, ensuring her feet were under her before letting her go. He kissed her briefly, then returned to his meeting with Robin, the young Tua De spy working for him.

The spy and MacLir were hunting for the magic pig that kept all the immortals from aging. Usually kept on an island off the coast of Ireland, It had been stolen last year and was still missing. Luckily, right before Pig was stolen, MacLir had stockpiled the magic ham and turned it into jerky. However, even rationing the jerky, if Pig could not be found soon, everyone would start aging again, and the oldest fairies would die.

Piper didn't want to get caught in the discussion on the bench. There was no room for her to sit anyway, so she drifted to the ship's side. She was surprised to find a friend ducked out of sight, seemingly eavesdropping.

"Fia! What are you doing lurking down there?" Piper asked.

"I never lurk," said the childish voice of the sea dragon, its head rising higher out of the water to speak with her. The sun lit the dragon's teal and emerald scales attractively, showing the hints of a purple hue.

"I haven't seen you in a while," said Piper. In fact, she rarely saw the creature who had pulled her into this world of magic.

Solid black protruding eyes tilted toward Piper, then over to the talking men. "You should read Robin's matches," suggested Fia.

Piper was intrigued. She knew Fia had magic somehow similar to hers, able to see flashes into the future. The sea dragon had never suggested Piper use her power before, but Fia had not led her wrong so far.

As casually as possible, she stared at Robin before looking away, preparing for the mental pictures she sensed coming. In the first vision, she saw Robin talking to a girl at an airport. At Dublin Airport, she was sure of it. He offered her an arm, and they left together. Transitioning to the second vision, she watched them both in the faerie tunnels, talking, in perhaps... Robin's room? She only caught a few words before the third snippet of their relationship was shown to her. Robin and the unknown woman playing with a toddler.

She always got a sense of the urgency for when the person she read would meet a person they could fall in love with. This meeting was urgent, so he'd need to arrive at the airport soon. Probably in the next couple of hours.

In mulling over the middle part of the vision, the words of the conversation came back to her... and gave her an idea. A mad—but possible—idea.

"Now time to inform the lucky groom," she told Fia, who nodded and slipped back into the waves.

Piper returned to the cabin to gather a stack of cash. MacLir always had a ton of it on hand and never cared what she spent it on. Approaching the two men, she said, "MacLir, could you do me a favor? I can't reach the pan on the tall shelf. Could you do it for me?"

MacLir glanced at her suspiciously. She never talked this much in front of strangers, and her voice was overly loud and bubbly, almost imitating Fia's tone and style.

"Sure," he replied. "Which pan?"

"Any pan. Actually, get down all the pans. Now would be great! Thanks!"

MacLir gazed at her for another moment, a smile twitching the corner of his lips, but he went. As soon as he left, Piper sat in his seat and leaned toward Robin. Her fake cheery tone evaporated, and she said, "I have a favor to ask."

"Anything for the Goddess of Love! Maybe you'll finally agree to point me in the right direction one day."

Piper ignored his quip. "Will you help or not?"

"My initial offer stands. How can I serve?"

Piper described the person Robin could meet at the airport and handed him all the money. "Spend as much time with her as possible, and make sure she doesn't leave the island, even if you have to pay for all of her expenses."

Copying MacLir's suspicious stare, he said, "I doubt you get so personally involved in everyone's love life. So what are you up to?"

Piper stared at her hands, no emotion peeking through.

"Ah well, a beautiful and stylish brown-eyed girl is waiting for my gentlemanly assistance. Guess I'll be off now."

"Oh, wait. Also, be sure to visit the great faerie mound with her because…" Piper trailed off. She was not good at lying, as her demonstration with MacLir a moment ago proved, but she didn't want to give away what she'd seen. "The girl, she might be helpful in, um… your spy work." There. That was believable, and Robin seemed to accept it.

This could be the answer, and with any luck, it might work.

Amy

"I'm leaving. Just so you know," said Amy.

"But why, Amalia? It's your sister's birthday, and she has not even arrived yet!" Her mother was frosting a cake and didn't bother to glance at her.

Amy cringed at her mother's insistence on calling her Amalia, especially when she'd made it clear she preferred a shortened version. Deciding not to start that argument again, she answered her mother's question. "Some small child leaked on my skirt, and it's not my fault Elena is late for her own party." Amy experienced another wave of annoyance at having been handed a cousin's infant to tend—without a please or thank you—and having to return home to clean up. She might not even come back to the tedious social gathering of her extended family.

She waited impatiently for her mother to let her go, but the harried woman often forgot to finish conversations, especially with her middle children. She bustled out of the kitchen, shouting, "Luna! I ran out of frosting! I need you to make more, please."

Taking her mother's inattention as her cue to leave, Amy hurried out of the kitchen unhindered, wondering if she would act like her mother one day too. She appeared similar to her mother, or rather, a younger version. All her sisters had the same oval brown face, shoulder-length wavy dark hair, and brown eyes. Unlike her mother and sisters, her eyebrows were plucked into a trendy arch, and her charming smile was covered in the perfect shade of lipstick. Today she was not smiling.

Ambling down a gentle slope from her grandparent's house to the only house she'd ever lived in, she enjoyed the view of crop fields far in the distance, catching a whiff of the stables. While a lovely place to grow up, lately she'd been itching for more. If she was honest with herself, it wasn't just recently. She couldn't remember a time she had not wanted adventure out in the wider world. When she was restless one early memory always flashed in her mind. Watching a spinning globe of the planet in her first classroom and wondering what it would be like to visit every place on earth.

Was life really about becoming an adult only to settle into married bliss with a farmer and become a mother? Nothing about motherhood appealed to her. From giving birth to changing diapers the whole process seemed unnecessarily messy. In this last year finishing highschool she'd decided it would be much better to stay free than become trapped in marriage and children. Free to be herself without anyone weighing her down. If she succeeded in becoming a travel writer she could travel the world. She could become anything. Not according to her family, but what did they know? They'd lived together on this farmland for three generations and planned to continue the tradition. When she moved away she'd miss her horse, but not her family.

Her mental meandering was cut short at the sight of the teen at the crossroads. She'd have to walk right past him since it was too late to avoid the confrontation using a different path. She sighed inwardly and followed the dusty road.

"Hello, Drew," Amy said hesitantly when she got closer.

Leaning against the fence in as manly a pose as he could manage, he pulled his hat low. "Good evening, Amy," he said in a fake deep voice.

She pressed lips tight to hold back a laugh. The other farm kids their age often picked on Drew, so Amy had always been kind to him. Of course, that backfired on her. Oh, here it comes.

"Amy," he said passionately and fell to his knees. "Will you marry me?"

His outstretched hand held a ring, which for the fifth time this month, Amy did not take. "Drew, we've been through this before. I'm not going to date you, much less marry you. We are related cousins somehow—which is weird—and I'm not attracted to you. This needs to stop." Given the circumstances, she'd said it as kindly as she could, but her tone was much firmer than the last four refusals.

"That's not reason enough to prevent destiny!" Dew whined in his natural higher-pitched voice. "I know after we kiss, you'll see. You'll feel differently."

He slipped in the mud in trying to rise, and his white cowboy hat fell off. He was pathetic sitting in the muck, so Amy grabbed his hat and gave him a hand to haul him to his feet. Big mistake. He took the opportunity of holding her hand to kiss it. Then, as if he could not help himself, he kept kissing all the way up, his scraggly goatee scraping along her arm.

"Knock it off," she yelled, yanking her hand out of his grasp and marching away from him. She ignored the familiar scene of fenced cattle on either side of her, still fuming about his audacity.

The sunset faded, causing dreary dusk to settle on the land. Hearing footsteps, she looked behind her and sighed at the sight of Drew following like a puppy. Or, maybe more of a stalking predator.

"Uh-oh, not a puppy," she muttered as he began to run.

She sprinted for a moment, but had no hope of outrunning him in her tight party dress, so she stood her ground. Drew stopped in confusion.

Saying the first thing that came to mind she announced, "I have your hat!"

He advanced with a glint in his eyes. "Yes," he squeaked out.

Quickly formulating a plan, she shifted her constricting skirt out of the way while saying invitingly, "Come get your hat." She held out his hat, her heart beating wildly.

One more step, and Drew was in range. She lifted the skirt to her knees, and while Drew's hungry eyes flicked to his hat, her leg shot up and kicked him in the groin, as her dad had taught her to do.

Drew fell hard, but she didn't pause to watch. Kicking off her shoes, she sprinted toward her family's farmhouse. She firmly believed she could not be harmed and would outrun him to get to safety. When she pictured this outcome, a burst of speed came from nowhere, and she dashed away.

When she reached the doorway, she peered over her shoulder and could make out his figure jogging toward her, although somewhat erratically. She flew through the shadowy main floor, locking all the doors and windows. The rattling sound of the locked front door knob sent her zipping upstairs and she slammed the bedroom door behind her.

The view from her window showed the entire front yard, and Drew knew it. He backed up until he could see her, grinning wolfishly in the dying light. Amy had never seen him as threatening and admitted she was scared as he pounded against the first floor windows one by one.

Eventually, he glared at her bedroom window again in obvious frustration, then limped away. Relief flooded through her so quickly that she got a headache.

Laying down in an attempt to settle her racing heart, she wondered what she could do about this. What if he chased her again tomorrow? She never believed he'd actually harm her, they'd known each other their whole lives, but that belief was shaken today. What would he have done tonight if he had caught her?

CHAPTER 2

Amy

"Where you wanna go?" the woman southern-drawled. She was standing behind an airline ticket counter, fingers hovering over the keys of a computer, ready to send Amy anywhere.

She'd saved money for getting settled in the city for her writing degree, but a daydream she couldn't get out of her head was a gap year in Europe. It had always sounded amazing to travel for a year when she was done with high school but before college started. Not that her mother was supportive of college, but Amy's sister Clara had always encouraged her to dream big.

Often, Clara was more of a parent to her than anyone else. Clara put her to bed as a child and was there when she had nightmares. It was Clara she turned to for advice when boys began flirting with her. Clara had found Amy after the party, still anxious from her run-in with Drew.

It was Clara who gave Amy the rest of the money needed for the gap year they'd planned out together one afternoon. Then helped her pack, and—ignoring her mother's protests—dropped Amy off at the airport. So, where did she want to go? The place didn't matter so much as her experiences there. She braced herself, remembering Clara's words, "Be bold."

Her daydream was really happening. A whole year between highschool and college to discover what she wanted from life. To experience travel before she committed herself to a writing career. In the time it took to fly over the ocean, she'd be staying in youth hostels in Italy, France, and Spain. Perhaps she should start in Spain?

"One-way ticket to Spain, please."

"I can give you a cheaper ticket to Ireland, and it's easy as pie to make your way from Ireland to Spain. Or, you can stay in Ireland for a few days and see some sights."

Ireland had never been added to her list when fantasizing about classic European historic sites, but she had to admit she was intrigued. Now, a bonus adventure was being offered by this added stop, so with a heady sense of freedom, she announced, "Book me a ticket to Ireland."

"Sure thing, honey. Enjoy your flight!"

The flight was surprisingly uneventful, ebbing away some of her initial bravery. Amy reminded herself she was anywhere except on her family farm. That was amazing, but as she ambled toward the airport's exit door, she stopped in view of it. Beyond was a whole country she had done no research about. Excitement shifted to worry. Her heart was pounding as she realized how alone she was for the first time in her life. She could not catch a full breath as the crowd flowed around her, uncertain of her next steps.

Amy focused on a captivating man only a few feet away from her. Spinning in slow circles and scanning the crowd. His khaki pants and oversized cream sweater looked comfy on his slim frame. He stopped spinning when his bright green eyes met hers and her heart skipped a beat.

"You look as lost as I feel," she said to him.

His curly hair flopped adorably over his forehead. "Are you lost?" he asked in an almost Irish accent.

Amy was never shy to talk to people, but still adrift in the gaze of this handsome man, she took a moment to find her voice. "A bit lost, I suppose."

"Where are you trying to find?"

"I'm going to Spain, and I could continue my travels now…" her voice trailed off as she glanced again at the exit door, "but I was thinking about touring here for a few days before leaving. Do you know any good places to stay?"

"It would be a tragedy for you to fly south without seeing any of Ireland but the airport. My friend owns a hotel. You could stay there for free, and I could show you around the city."

She eyed this man offering assistance. She was no stranger to boys wanting to spend time with her, but she was not getting any warning signs from his tone or friendly smile. Be bold, her sister had said. Making the decision to follow her gut, she believed everything would be fine. She chose to view the situation as lucky how easily she'd found a trustworthy tour guide. She thrust out a hand saying, "My name is Amy."

"I"m Robin." The touch of his hand on hers sent tingles zinging through her body.

"It's nice to meet you, Robin. I don't know what I would have done today without your help."

On the taxi ride to the hotel, it was natural to accept his dinner invitation and suggestion to wander in the local public gardens. Amy wondered about that easy faith in his intentions. What was it about him causing her to trust him? Perhaps it was his gentle smile, their comfortable silence for the rest of the taxi ride, or the casual conversation over dinner. He had not tried to get her alone, ensuring they were surrounded by people while keeping a respectful distance.

Now strolling the busy garden with him, her thoughts broke away from their chat as she considered staying a few more days. Nothing was pulling her in any other direction. Even more interesting was how Robin offered to pay for all sightseeing during her trip here. As if he didn't want her to leave too soon.

"Away with the fairies again?" asked Robin.

Amy came back to reality, noticing Robin had been talking, but was now peering thoughtfully at her. Oops and drat! "Oh, I um... What?" she asked, thoroughly bewildered.

"Away with the fairies. Staring off into space."

"Ah. Yes. I was… thinking."

"Sorry if I distracted you." They continued to meander along the path leading to a pond surrounded by old trees. "I was saying this garden was my favorite place to visit when I was a child."

"I can see why. I love it here. It's charming," said Amy, trying to ease into the only uncomfortable topic they'd discussed. "So, about your offer…"

"Yeah?" he asked hopefully.

"Robin, it's sweet, but I don't want you to waste your money on me."

"I would do it gladly. Do you want to stay for a while?"

She did want to stay, but how to say it? "I would like to see more of Ireland with you. However, I insist on paying my own way for anything expensive."

Robin's bright smile was contagious and Amy smiled back at him when he said, "We'll see. Let's start tomorrow, I know a great place where we can eat dinner."

After another ten minutes of meandering the gardens, he took her hand, glancing sideways at her with a nervous smile to check if she welcomed the contact. She returned his smile as a tiny part of her nagged how it was all too soon, but the rest of her ignored that part, enjoying the contact of their warm hands. What was travel for, if not to live differently than you live at home? See new sights and have a vacation fling. She knew all the boys in her town, and it was fascinating to enjoy attraction for someone she didn't grow up with.

They parted at the front gates of the garden because he said he was late for work, and she assured him she was confident she could make it back to the hotel from here.

"I had a nice time, Amy. I'm excited for tomorrow night's date."

"Yep, me too," she said, smiling at his eagerness.

"Brilliant." He kissed the back of her hand in a charmingly old-fashioned gesture and waved once as he jogged away. She waved back and could hardly wait to see him again soon.

Wandering slowly under the streetlamps back to the hotel, she imagined a life full of events like those of today. Flying to unfamiliar countries, eating at delightful restaurants, touring historic gardens, meeting handsome strangers, and sleeping in cozy hotels. A life full of adventure? Then writing all about it for people to live vicariously through her experiences. It was an intoxicating idea that she wanted more every day.

Lucky

Sitting in the dark for hours was not helping his mood. Lucky was hidden in a shadow, something he'd been doing more often in these uncertain times. Today he was watching the faerie entrance. Waiting for a boy MacLir had decided to trust based solely on Brigit's recommendation. The boy was late.

After a short reign as king and during Lucky's hundreds of years living in both the faerie mounds and the human realm, he served and loved his youthful foster father, MacLir. In a completely different way, he was starting to realize he loved the healer, Brigit. At the moment, he was cursing them both for leaving him here in the dark underground faerie tunnel.

If Robin was not here soon, Lucky would have to leave without him. The two of them were planning to spy on the meeting of the so-called rebels and find out more about what they were trying to accomplish with their random attacks.

Lucky had never played at being a spy before. He'd considered wearing less flashy clothing, but discovered he didn't own any. Good thing his clothes were already dark, from his fitted jewel-toned buttoned shirts to his black vest, sturdy boots, and stylish long coat.

Even his blue-black hair would blend nicely into the dim corner he'd used to watch the last meeting. His pale face was the only problem, but he'd practiced pulling a hat low and his coat up, so only his green eyes showed.

A bump from the shimmering entrance caught his attention, and he watched Robin stand and dust off his pants. An ungraceful landing from the travel tunnels was not an impressive start.

"You're late." Lucky took pleasure in watching the boy jump. A sign his camouflage was working perfectly.

"Ah, Lugh. Sorry about the delay. Are we still in time to get to the meeting?"

"Barely. Let's go." Lucky strode away, leaving Robin to catch up. His haste was partly to cover the slight cringe at hearing his actual name. Even if Lugh was still his most popular name, he wasn't that person anymore. His modern name and clothing gave him a sense of starting fresh. As if he could create another life. Maybe with Brigit.

Lucky led Robin in the direction of the meeting room. This was the second of these not exactly secret meetings, but it was still invitation only. If you knew where to gather, it was assumed you'd been invited. He had found out the location of most of the meetings and scouted ahead for places to hide. Because, as a recognizable friend of MacLir, Lucky had been staying in the shadows during these meetings.

Before anyone could see him or connect him to Robin, he flashed away with a small pop, disappearing from Robin's side. Then, reappearing in the deepest shadow he'd seen in the outer chamber, he watched everyone milling and chatting in the high-ceilinged faerie mound before the meeting started.

The faerie tunnels were close enough to the surface that above ground this would be seen as a small hill, also known as a faerie mound. Anyone who called it that would be correct. Faerie mounds in Ireland appeared as grass-covered hills dotting the landscape. Some were built as king's fortifications, others for a king's burial, and legends had formed around them. It was said, if they were desecrated, the fairies would enforce a curse on the trespasser. While not wholly accurate, the consequences could be harmful to humans.

Fairies came in all shapes and sizes, but this crowd was all the human-sized fae known as the Tuatha Dé Danann, and the gathering was larger than he'd expected. One of the attendees made eye contact with him before he could finish getting his coat into place around his pale cheeks. Lucky recognized him as one of the fanatical supporters of the new would-be king. Worse, the fan recognized him in return.

"Lugh Lámfada?" The man's jaw dropped to see the ex-warrior king skulking in a crack in a cave. Lucky watched the man shift from confused when whispering his name in shock, to recognition and anger at what he could be doing there. "You… you… you work for MacLir!" The man glanced around, shifting from foot to foot, deciding what to do about this potential threat.

Lucky pulled magic from around him, from the soil of the walls and the trees above. Power flowed into Lucky from the island itself.

"You're here to ruin everything," the man mumbled. "I have to tell—" At that moment, the man made the mistake of glancing back at Lucky one last time and was caught in Lucky's glowing green gaze. The man's mouth snapped shut, and his eyes went glassy.

"You don't see me. You never saw me. Now, walk away." Lucky let his eyes fade quickly, in case anyone else noticed. The man drunkenly stepped backward in a daze and meandered through the crowd. Lucky was quicker getting his coat in place over his cheeks on this second attempt and shrunk deeper into his hiding place.

Finally able to watch and protect Robin again, Lucky scanned the noisy crowd for the boy and was shocked to see him talking to Brigit. Straining to hear, he caught part of their conversation.

"I had no idea there was a gathering here today," said Brigit.

"Then… what are you doing here?" Robin asked suspiciously, closely watching his mentor and friend.

"One of the High Court members asked me to meet him here briefly. To discuss a bit of important policy before our next court meeting," said Brigit airily. "What are you doing at this event? I'm not even sure what it's for."

"It's a political event, and I'm here covering it. To write a piece on it for work," replied Robin. His tone seemed to completely trust what Brigit had said, but Lucky knew her better. Her guarded eyes would not meet Robin's. She was hiding something.

"Oh, so you got the job with the Tirnanog Tabloid? I'll let you go if I'm keeping you from work." Brigit hastily hurried away with a cheery wave.

Lucky continued to monitor Robin as he cycled through attendees in the crowd, gathering opinions and writing quotes in an open notebook. Maybe it was a Tua De magic talent the boy was unaware of, but people trusted him quickly, or perhaps it was simply his youthful charm. Lucky was a long way from a boyish young charm. He'd almost died at age forty before becoming immortal, so even his youthful genetics from his father's side could not completely hide his age.

Robin, another half Tuatha Dé Danann like himself, was more recently born, however the human side of his genes was not as strong. It barely showed through, so all the other Tua De in the room were happy to talk to him about their conspiracy theories.

Many people were excited about the option of a change in leadership. A new king after so many years of the last king. This group, though, was not filled with happy people. Until recently, these were what he'd considered the fringes of the population, pushing their outdated beliefs.

He wondered again what Brigit had been doing here. Maybe she was trying to find what was going on, like Robin, or perhaps she was telling the truth about her visit. Either way, she could not be an attendee. He didn't see how she would fit into this disgraceful crowd of ungrateful Tua De.

The doors opened, and many dozens of discontented fae streamed into the high ceiled room to cheer on their recently acquired leader. Lucky flashed from his current hiding place to one inside the meeting area, a deep crack in the natural cave wall he could hide in, but no one could see or reach him.

Amidst cheers and shouts of "Ian! Ian! Ian for King!" the king-to-be-hopeful strutted onto the low stage. Lucky had seen plays here in the past, but this was a very different performance he was watching today.

"Hello, friends!" Ian waved both hands at everyone in the crowd, a big smile on his doughy face lit by the stage lights above and around him. His fedora didn't match his suit jacket or the burgundy wool scarf he wore instead of a tie. Although, he resembled the other Tua De as odd in his appearance. With the time difference between realms, when fairies visited the human world, it could be decades between shopping trips. Human trends changed so quickly the faeries wore a mix of styles from many eras. On the other hand, Lucky lived mainly in the human world and took pride in his polished appearance.

Lucky wondered if this mess of clothes was a style Ian chose to appeal to the crowds supporting him. They were shouting again, with light from the stage creating odd angles and shadows across the many faces as they chanted, "Voiceless Pure! Voiceless Pure!"

Ian began his speech with a chilling shout, "My people! The Voiceless Pure! Humans will finally pay for their treachery!"

Lucky closed his eyes as his stomach did flips. So, it was true. He had heard whispers of its return, but not even at the last couple of meetings he'd managed to sneak into had anyone said the actual words. The Voiceless Pure. Not something common in the Tua De community since he was a child. Well before they all came to live underground in the elemental's realm.

Ian continued spouting nonsense during his short speech until it ended with, "A lot of Tua De know that MacLir has joined the humans against us." A bald lie that still got cheers from the crowd.

It was true MacLir often acted like an airheaded youth and was recently fascinated with a human girl, but the boy was serious about her. She'd been given powers and made immortal. Piper was not Tua De or even a faerie, but she was not exactly human anymore either. Besides, Piper was one human, and MacLir had always been on the Tua De's side.

Ian opened the meeting for questions, and Lucky hoped Robin was smart enough to keep his mouth shut. These were clearly questions from plants in the audience meant to boost Ian's image. Lucky had not managed to get close to the man, but knew his ego was enormous.

Someone in the crowd taunted Ian with the question, "If MacLir is against us, why did he rescue us? Why does he let us stay in his realm?" Lucky agreed with the sentiment, but shook his head at the stupidity of going against these people in their own gathering.

At first, Ian ignored the man, still rousing the crowd with his now-familiar phrase, "Our golden era is back!" Then, when the crowd exploded into chanting it back to him, Ian nodded to the two guards closest to the heckler.

The guards slipped through the mass of people and knocked the guy out, quietly dragging him away while Ian shouted, "We are making life better for our clans!"

CHAPTER 3

Piper

Piper turned the page of her novel, realized she didn't remember anything from the last page, and sighed. Putting a bookmark in the book, she stood from the bench and stretched. She didn't mind her own company, but had discovered there were limits. Having MacLir around, or spending time with Lucky, had become routine, but now she was alone more and more often. She shut her eyes tight as water splashed over her, followed by a thump on the deck. Joy rose in her chest as that could only mean one thing.

She opened her eyes to see MacLir, dripping wet, but smiling at her as he shook water out of his short blond hair. She used to get upset when she got damp, but after living for months on a ship, being a little damp occasionally was now part of life, even if she still didn't enjoy it.

MacLir moved forward for a hug and Piper braced, ready to get even more damp, but MacLir remembered in time. He paused to order the saltwater away from himself. It went. Zinging away in all directions and leaving him completely dry to give her a warm comforting hug. "I'm sorry, I think I've probably been gone for a while."

"You have. But I understand." She did understand. For one thing, he was desperately searching for his pig, but even more importantly, meandering in the ocean he lost all track of time and forgot he had people who relied on him. Who loved him. He always remembered eventually though, and that was what mattered.

She leaned toward him for a kiss and returned his grin. "Now that you are back, what should we do today!"

A sparkle lit his eyes. "I was thinking… the orphanage?"

Piper clapped her hands and bounced in place, "Yes! Yay! I have some new ideas, so let's get some supplies first."

Over the eras MacLir had taken in and raised several foster children, like Lucky, but as mound politics progressively turned against humans, more than a usual amount of half-human fae children were being abandoned. Piper loved that recently MacLir had purchased land in the human realm and built them a house with hallways of rooms. The selkies ran it, and the head cook of the faerie mounds sent the shunned children to it.

MacLir landed Wave Sweeper in the emerald grass on a low cliff, close to a large lone white house with a double peaked roof. On one side stretched the expanse of the ocean and on the other farmland as far as the eye could see. Not another house in sight for miles. At the end of the path down to the beach lazed a handful of seals. Humans would see them as typical gray seals found in Ireland, but Piper and everyone in this household could see their true color was blue. A sign they were not regular seals, but half Tua De shapeshifting selkies.

They were greeted at the door by Jimmy and Flora, a pair of six-year-old twins. "It's Piper!" squealed Flora. She raced away through every room in the house and her shouting drifted back to them, "Piper and MacLir are here!" Jimmy however only had eyes for MacLir. He wrapped his little arms as far around MacLir as they would go and beamed up at him. "You're back."

MacLir smiled warmly at the boy, set the shopping bags down, and sat on the floor between two tidy rows of shoes by the door. Grabbing the shoes of his little shadow, he began tying the laces together. "Those are my shoes, stop!" Giggled the boy.

MacLir only smiled again. "Would you like to hear a story?"

"Oh, yes please," answered Jimmy, settling on the ground as close as possible to MacLir so their knees almost touched. Other kids swarmed around them as they rushed in from various rooms and pounded down the stairs.

To many peals of laughter, and Piper's amusement, MacLir began the legend of the time he posed as a court magician and put the head of a dog on backwards. Meanwhile, one at a time, he tied together the laces of all fifteen pairs of shoes by the door. When he reached for the orphanage director's shoes, Jimmy broke into the end of the familiar story saying, "Noooo! Not those shoes."

"Why not these shoes?" MacLir raised an eyebrow.

"She's old and might get hurt!" said one child. Another added, "We love her!"

MacLir chuckled as the director swished into the room. "I appreciate the loyalty, kids. But I'm not so old that I can't withstand one of MacLir's tricks." The selkie in human form wore a short dress on her lean body, her mass of dark hair falling around her shoulders, and a toddler propped against her.

When Piper reached out, she received the toddler, cuddling him close, and leaving the director free to grin at MacLir, both hands on hips. "What is the plan for today?

Switching my salt with my sugar again? Or, a repeat of last time… rolling the visiting selkies in the water while they sleep?"

MacLir laughed as he replaced the director's shoes on the ground—with the laces tied together. "Neither. Apparently we have a calm day ahead of us planned by Piper. Baking and crafts."

The director rolled her eyes and headed up the stairs. Over her shoulder she added, "I'll believe it when I see it."

The children turned to Piper, excitement in their eyes. She picked up the bags and announced, "Let's make… cupcakes! To the kitchen!"

While the cupcakes were in the oven the older kids each got a tiny bowl of frosting to pick which color of food dye to add. It didn't escape Piper's notice that Jimmy and MacLir were whispering over their bowls, and when she glanced at them again she caught them dripping green dye into the milk jug.

Piper was not the only one to catch them in the act. "You're worse than the kids while you are here. Teaching them bad habits," sighed the director with a smile.

"Life is more interesting with a bit of fun," said MacLir, winking at Jimmy.

When not a crumb of the cupcakes remained, Piper gathered the last two shopping bags and led the group to the big tables in their dining room. She spread out paper in all colors and sizes and began showing them how to fold flying cranes, jumping frogs, boats, airplanes, and more.

She became suspicious when MacLir went quiet and watched out of the corner of her eye as he secretively folded paper after paper for ten minutes. Hiding his work by slipping the finished pieces in his lap. Piper kept an eye on him, and all the kids were whispering about what he could be doing. Finally he gathered all his folded paper into his hands and held it above his head victoriously, shouting, "Paper boats!" MacLir sprinted to the doorway. "I'll have to float them in the river all by myself… unless any of you are fast enough to catch me."

Chairs toppled and squeals of delight echoed in the room as a herd of children rushed after him to the entryway. Piper and Flora followed at a more sedate pace in time to see him standing outside the door, taunting the children with his arms full of paper. "Look! Look! All these wonderful boats. Hurry, hurry! You can't catch me." He acted as if he was going to run, but stayed to watch as all the children, who had slipped on their shoes to chase him, tripped on their tied laces and ended in a tangled heap on the doorstep.

Pleased and smug, MacLir could not contain his glee and collapsed on the ground roaring with laughter. The children kicked off their shoes to run outside, as barefoot as MacLir, and pounced on him, tickingly his sides and giggling. Then they gathered the boats and trooped off to the river, not a single shoe among them.

The toddler on Piper's hip grabbed her braid and tugged it. Piper gently removed the chubby fist from her hair and turned to Flora. "Well, more paper for us then?"

Flora nodded and took Piper's hand to lead her back to the dining hall. Piper's heart felt crushed at the thought she might never have her own tiny beings like these, which renewed her determination to find a way. She sometimes considered taking one of these children with her, but they were happy here with the house and life MacLir had built for them. After being around so many other kids, they might get lonely on the ship.

Sometimes she wished she could stay here to keep playing with the children, but after a few hours of so many people, it overwhelmed her. Even children she liked. In the meantime, visiting was nice, and one day she'd have her own child to bake with. They could come visit the orphanage together and play with the children, then head back to the nice quiet ship. She could see the future she wanted so clearly, almost like one of her visions. Now, all she needed to do was make it happen.

Amy

After a late-night out with Robin, dawn came sooner than Amy would have liked. She was woken by Robin pounding on the door. "Rise and shine, lazy bones!" he called. "Time to go!"

"I'm tired," she called back.

"Too bad," he said, laughing.

She could listen to his delightful laugh all day and had been enjoying everything about him on their day trips around Ireland. Her sleepy thoughts collided with her exhaustion from perhaps too much adventuring all week. So, since all was quiet for a few minutes, she quickly drifted back to sleep.

"Amy! We have travel time, are you coming? Open the door!"

"Coming. Yep," she said while yawning and pulling open the hotel door, remembering what she'd fallen asleep in a moment too late.

Glancing down, Amy caught sight of the black sports bra and tiny pink pajama shorts, took in Robin's playful grin, and shut the door in his face.

"I'll wait in the lobby," he said through the door.

She was fully awake now and grabbed at jeans and her running shoes. Adding a quick layer of light makeup, she hurried downstairs and found Robin flipping through travel guides in the empty lobby.

He had not said anything yet, but an awkwardness remained, so Amy decided to put the silly moment into per-spective. "You know, if I was in my bikini, you'd have seen even more of me."

"Do you want to go swimming?" he asked enthusiastically.

"No! I don't know how to swim. I was trying to explain, ugg." Rarely embarrassed, her ears were going hot, so she gave up and laughed with Robin as he opened the hotel's front door for her.

At the harbor, they boarded a small fishing boat to ferry them over to an island. The captain piloted from a tiny front cabin, while Robin and Amy sat in seats at the back of the boat. Robin tapped his knee, thinking, and finally said, "Can I tell you a short story?"

The wind whipped Amy's hair so she could hardly see anything, and she was glad she had not bothered styling it this morning. She shrugged. Might as well listen if she couldn't see, so she bumped shoulders with him and replied, "Go for it."

"Long ago, the Tuatha Dé Danann were a magical civilization in Ireland. Skilled in art, science, poetry, and magic. Compared to humans, they had a long life span, but they could be killed. After arriving, they ruthlessly took control of Ireland from the locals in a series of battles. When the next group of humans arrived to conquer Ireland, the Tua De were defeated."

Amy laughed at the random tidbit of local legend. She'd seen something in one of the gift shops about an ancient group called the Tuatha Dé Danann. "Okay. How long ago was this?" Amy asked.

"Something like three thousand years ago, or so. Why?"

She shrugged again and hoped this story had a point.

"When defeated in the last battle, the Tua De were given two options. To mix with the humans or be given half of Ireland to live in. They chose to stay separate, but it was a trick. They were given the underground half of Ireland. As the conquerors herded everyone into a deep cave to die,

Manannán MacLir, the sea god, helped them cross over into the Otherworld, or Sidhe Realm. It was already there with all the faeries, elves, gnomes, leprechauns, and other fae creatures. The Tuatha Dé Danann fit right in and still live there today."

When researching all the countries she wanted to visit, she noticed surprising similarities in their folklore. Many people suggested they were based on fact, but that didn't mean any were true. She held back an eye roll. "So, you are saying faeries still live in Ireland. Pardon me if I remain skeptical."

"Skeptical is good. It shows you are close to belief!"

At her snort, he tickled her side, and they both laughed. Amy liked his casual touch and resettled closer to him.

The boat slowed to edge around a corner of an island and stopped to idle within view of a stone castle. The captain stepped out of his wind shelter and gave a practiced tour guide speech about the island and the castle.

Amy interrupted him when she glimpsed movement in the water at a distance. "What's that in the water?"

"Gray seals, miss," said the captain. "They are regularly here or hangin' about nearby."

"Wow!" Amy surged to her feet for a better view, standing on the fishing boat's edge at a gap in the rails. In the choppy waves, she overbalanced, slipping on the wet deck and splashing into the cold water below.

CHAPTER
4

Amy

While sinking, she considered how valuable swimming lessons would have been. She'd played in the water a time or two, but living in the desert, ponds and pools were for entertainment, not to hone a necessary skill.

She shut her eyes tight and hoped Robin would save her soon, when something brushed against her leg. She tried not to think about any movies featuring deadly animals in the water. It bumped her again, and this time she kicked blindly, but went still when the dark, mysterious shape pushed her through the water toward the surface. Sweet fresh air filled her lungs, and she scanned the waterline to see her rescuer. It was a huge blue-black seal.

The boat had not moved, but the seal's prodding made the land closer, and Robin was swimming toward her. The seal continued to help her float and Robin called, "Keep going!"

Another seal bobbed out of the water next to her. They made a raft between the two of them to carry her to the island. She was deposited on the beach right before two seals dropped Robin off. All the seals galumphed onto the shore nearby and stretched out in the sun.

Robin settled Amy, sitting her down on the mixed rock and sand, and gave her a tight hug. "Are you alright?"

"They are amazing. So beautiful. They worried me at first, but they are tame for wild animals. And such a mesmerizing shade of blue."

"So, you can see them as blue?" asked Robin.

Amy laughed. "I see them as blue because they are blue." She fluffed his matted hair, bringing back the bits of wild curl she liked so much.

"You must be faerie touched to see the seal's true nature and I wondered if you'd be able to see them by now."

She narrowed her eyes at him. She wanted to watch the seals and enjoy the warm sun drying their clothes. Instead, he was back to chattering about legends. "Problem, Robin. I've never met a faerie."

"You may not have known."

"Trust me. If I met a faerie, I'm sure it's something I'd notice." He was talking gibberish, but Amy suddenly remembered the odd behavior of the seal though. "The seals, they rescued us."

"Yes," said Robin with a shrug.

"I'm confused. Why would seals help us?"

"They are fae too. Selkies, actually. Uh, oh. Look behind you."

"Hi, Robin. And hey, hey pretty lady," said a voice from beside her. She expected to see another tourist, and instead, a naked man lay stretched sideways in the sand next to her. His head was propped on one hand, his other hand on his hip, everything on full display, showcasing a strong swimmer's body.

Amy jumped, landing practically in Robin's lap. "What? Where did you come from?"

"Hello to you too," he said with a wink. "You know, kicking me when I was simply trying to rescue you was uncalled for. So, I'm here for an apology kiss."

"Away with you," said Robin, laughing. "No kiss is on offer, but she's sorry about kicking you, right?"

"Right," stammered Amy.

"Apology accepted." The man's skin shimmered as he morphed back into a blue-black seal too fast for Amy's eyes to follow. He twisted around to get on his belly, then humped along the beach to rejoin the others.

"What? What… just happened?" Amy asked, her gaze flicking between the seals and Robin.

"You can see them, their true nature, so you are already fae-touched, marked as a friend of faeries. I tried to do it, but was not sure it worked… because I'm fae too. A Tua De."

Magic was real. Selkies were real. She could almost wrap her mind around that, but Robin was a faerie? One from his story? She tried to think back on the details, but all she could remember him saying was something about three thousand years ago. "How old are you?"

"I'm not sure, the fae don't count age the same way since time passes differently between the realms. I'm young though. I mean a younger generation, so probably close to your age. Also, as half-human, I was allowed to leave the mounds and live in the mortal world. Oh, and I have a bit of magic, but mine is common. I can move small stuff." He reached out a hand, and a few rocks rolled sideways, knocking into other rocks.

The shock of seeing the selkie transform combined with her awe of watching Robin do magic was too much for her, and she kept the conversation going to cover her shock. "Rolling rocks? That's not useful," said Amy teasingly, a playful smile wrinkling her eyes.

"Does it have to have a use?" Robin replied, tickling her side again, making her squeal and bat at him. "Actually, speaking of usefulness, I wonder if you could help me with something."

"Sure." She agreed automatically, but wondered if she should have got details first.

"Remember when I told you I'm a writer? I've agreed to use my writing skills as a cover. I'm sort of spying on a group of other faeries," he said proudly. "Maybe you could help too."

Amy's mind whirled, trying to take in too much too soon. She loved that Robin was a writer too, but now he was both a faerie and a spy? The first one almost fit him, the second one not at all. Of course, not appearing like a spy would make him a good spy. Or maybe not, if he was bragging about it.

It was all too much, and she needed to think about it later, so she decided to change the subject. "Why did we come to this island?"

His cheerful smile faltered at her abrupt question. "To see the seals. I thought you'd enjoy them… and maybe they would be a good introduction to the magical community."

Amy took a deep breath. Be bold, she reminded herself. She could not turn away from more adventure than she'd ever dreamed possible. She leaned over and kissed Robin's cheek. Reassuring him, and perhaps herself, she said, "I am enjoying the seals… and you."

"That's lovely to hear." He held her close, and they watched the splash of seals playing in the water between them and the harbor.

Amy

After a long night swirling the concepts of Robin's story in her mind, she finally decided she believed. Remembering his demonstration of moving the rocks was more impressive than she'd admitted at the time, so the following day, she was ready for dazzling magic. Instead, he'd led them to the same gardens they'd visited on her first day.

"Why are we back here?" she asked.

"The gardens are the nearest hidden entrance to take us to the Otherworld."

"Are there different entrances?" Amy wondered how many she had passed during her days here in this extraordinary country.

"Loads. We are visiting the largest mound on this trip. It's the location of the faerie kitchens, the Great Room for feasting, and my old bedroom."

They passed the pond where they'd first held hands. Was it only a week ago? Finally, they struck out into the forest. Well off the path, between two gnarled old trees was a shimmery area, as if Amy saw the grass through a heatwave.

"Here we are," announced Robin cheerfully.

"This is the entrance to faerie land? Why don't other people see it here?"

"They do, if they are faerie-touched."

Apprehension about this plan skittered across Amy's mind for the first time. She resisted the urge to back away from the portal but asked, "Why did you have me check out of the hotel?"

"Since we are staying overnight, we won't be back in the mortal realm for weeks."

"Whoa, an extreme time difference." Amy wanted to hesitate, to wait here until she was sure this was the right step, but how often was the opportunity to visit fairies going to come up? All those years stuck at the farm, finding what small adventures she could, and dreaming of more. All those lectures from her mother about farm life being the safe choice. What was the point of being alive without living? Be bold, she reminded herself for what seemed like the hundredth time. Throwing caution to the wind, she gripped Robin's outstretched hand, and they stepped into the center of the shimmering circle.

In the blink of an eye, they were no longer in the garden, but instead slipping quickly down a hard-packed dirt tunnel. Sometimes the pitch dark slide was so vertical it almost felt like falling. Amy gripped Robin's hand as wind both whipped past them and pushed them along, adding an eerie, haunting moan to the journey.

The time in the tunnel took only moments before Amy's hand was pulled from Robin's and they were dropped onto a cave floor. A dim glow from above added to the gloom and left dark shadows in corners. Amy glanced behind from her position on the floor, expecting to see the tunnel opening from this side, but there was only a solid dirt wall.

"Bags of potatoes! Sorry, I still need practice landing on my feet." Robin quickly stood, dusting himself off, and offered Amy a hand. She not only grasped it, but used it to pull herself close to him. He took the opportunity to hug her tightly, and she fit perfectly in the circle of Robin's arms.

"Are you okay? You're shaking like a leaf."

"It was all so fast," she mumbled, "And where did the portal go?" Her heart was beating rapidly, and she wondered if she'd made a mistake coming here.

Robin eased her away and slung her pack over his shoulder, saying, "I'm sorry if that was unexpected, I should have warned ya. We were actually traveling across quite a bit of land."

She swallowed a few times, trying to find her voice, rubbing clammy palms on her jeans. Robin smiled reassuringly when she failed to reply and led her through a tunnel, then around two corners. The smell of the mostly dirt hallways was pleasant. Like spring farm soil back home. Earthy. It calmed her, but she was surprised again by the next curve in the path.

The dirt of the tunnel gave way to a vast stone cavern. The ceiling was visible, but surprisingly high. The whole place was covered in, well, creatures. Scenes she'd only seen in movies, dreams, or nightmares, but nothing she'd ever believed was real. They were eating in groups on the ground, at the dozens of tables, or off in darker corners.

Robin picked his way through a group of chattering short pointy-eared elves, but left space when guiding her around a circle of trolls noisily crunching on carrots. An orange feral cat with furry wings ran across their path, claws out, chased by an enraged wingless calico who was hissing and snarling.

The chaos was overwhelming as they moved farther into the great room. The cacophony of loud voices speaking many languages, combined with barks, squeals, and squawks, made Amy edgy. She was not usually so overwhelmed by sound. She wondered if this was what everyday life was like for Clara, her extremely sensitive autistic sister.

They finally reached the group of human-shaped beings on the far side of the room, all surprisingly tall with pale faces and brown hair. They were dressed in clothes from different eras, a mix of medieval to modern jeans and everything in between.

They didn't look entirely human, though. Something about how they stood or how they stared at her was eerie. She glanced at Robin. His posture had shifted, and it scared her that he seemed more like them now.

Piper

"I finally got a message back from Robin." MacLir narrowed his eyes at Piper, his fake anger hindered by a teasing smile. "He says he's busy on an errand… for you."

The ocean breeze plucked strands of hair from her braid and tickled her neck with them as she tried to think of a reply. "Not for me. Not exactly. I pointed him in the right direction. He's busy falling in love right now." At least, that's what Piper hoped he was doing.

"He's supposed to focus on mound politics, but I suppose falling in love is more fun," said MacLir. He pulled Piper off the bench to dance around the deck. She laughed with him. Her boy was so silly sometimes. She reveled again in how wonderful it was having someone nearby who also understood the joy of being ridiculous together.

Startling them both, Fia's giant head leaned over the ship's edge. MacLir instinctively edged himself in front of Piper as her protector. The only other time the sea dragon had come this far onto the deck was when Fia bit Piper, injecting poison directly into her bloodstream. The poison was supposedly a gift—a way to speak with her new cat and other animals—but it showed how differently the sea dragon thought of both friends and gifts.

MacLir had once mentioned how he could understand all creatures in or around the sea, except Fia. So, between Fia's otherness and the attack on Piper, MacLir had grown more cautious around the dragon. In fact, Piper realized the sea dragon rarely appeared when MacLir was around.

"You must go to the faerie kitchens. Now. Don't go in. Stay outside and in the human world. Go now." The dragon's bubbly voice was still childish, but had a serious undertone giving her instructions urgency. "I must go." Within seconds Fia was a speck in the distance.

CHAPTER 5

Amy

"Why am I going by myself? Actually, why am I going at all?"

"A friend said… you'd be helpful. With the spying. She saw it in a vision." Robin's confidence visibly faltered as he added, "I think."

Amy was not at all sure about becoming a spy. Yearning for the excitement of travel and new places was one thing. Undercover work was a completely different type of adventure. Worse, she was starting to get the sense that perhaps Robin was new to spying, and maybe she should not get involved. Although… his plan was so basic, what could go wrong?

"So, you want me to wander into a secret meeting—acting as if I'm lost   on the off chance I might hear something useful? How will I know what's important? How dangerous are these people?"

"Probably not too dangerous. They are politicians. Good luck. I shouldn't be seen around here, but I'll be right around the corner waiting for you. Remember to go right at both forks in the tunnel." Robin gave her a double thumbs up and dashed away.

"Get back here," Amy whispered, but he was gone. Shocked that Robin had left her alone in the darkest tunnel they'd been in yet, she was frozen in place with indecision. She could follow him, do as he wanted, or ask the next person she saw for directions out of this mad place. Robin had been so gentlemanly up to this point, she didn't know what to think of him now.

Gathering her thoughts she chose an option. Deciding to go after Robin and ask him what was going on, she hesitated when deep voices reached her from around a corner and she paused to listen.

"The Burren?"

"Yes, settling into new quarters."

"What about the ceremony?"

"We'll do it below the dolmen stone."

Amy jumped when a voice from in front of her said, "What are you doing here?"

She whipped her head up to see two men towering over her and tried to remember her cover story. Was it something about being lost? Her mind was blank as the men continued to stare.

"I recognize you. You came in with Robin. So, you want little magical babies, huh?" one man said nastily.

Her lost voice returned at his assumptions about her motives. Not bothering to put together an explanation about being lost, she demanded, "Explain that comment to me. Now."

"You humans always want our magic babies. You find out about us and want your baby to live forever. But no matter how many babies you have, nothing you create with a half-human like Robin will be allowed to live among us."

Amy understood she might not have a firm grasp on the situation. However, she also knew an insult when she heard one. Or several. "I'm happy to inform you I don't want any babies! Robin's or otherwise. Even if I had a child, I would not let it live in this shabby hole with you arrogant idiots!"

She shifted to walk around them, but one man side-stepped into her way. "Let's take her to Ian, we don't know why she's here."

"I'm not letting you take me anywhere."

"You don't have a choice." The fae ground out.

"Drop dead!"

The man's face went even more pale than his companions. He staggered backward as she stomped away from them, ignoring the commotion behind her. The further she got from the meeting, the more she remembered the plan. All she had to do was ask for directions and they would have been less suspicious. Maybe spying was not for her.

With her temper cooled off, she noticed she didn't recognize this bend in the cave. Then, with a sinking feeling, she realized she'd lost her way. She had taken a wrong fork in her angry haze. She collapsed on the ground and hugged her knees. Echoes of instructions from many camping trips said it was better to stay put when lost, rather than continue wandering in possibly the wrong direction. When she didn't come right back, Robin would go searching for her.

This part of the tunnel was damp. When she rested her hands on the ground, she discovered it was mud. The rest of her anger melted into fear. Trying to stay calm, she called, "Robin!"

The sound did not carry. The dripping ceiling was the only noise. Her imagination went to work. She remembered the giant trolls from the big cave and wondered if they ate humans. Would one of them come to find her here alone and crunch on her bones? She pictured the ghosts of its victims living in the walls. What if they started seeping out? A bit of glowing white began to radiate from one spot in the ceiling. "I'm being ridiculous," she said aloud and the glow winked out. Hearing her own voice helped calm her. "Robin!" she called again, louder this time.

What if creatures in the tunnels were attracted to her voice? Like… a huge cave spider. Were those real or only in movies? She imagined a huge spider, drawn by her last shout, was already on its way. Motion at the end of the tunnel caught her eye just as she remembered giant spiders did not exist. Besides, nothing was visible when focusing her gaze in that direction… so she must have imagined it. Although small spiders liked dark places, right?

Amy remembered the time spiders had hatched in the barn back home. They were everywhere. Little spiders were very possible. She pictured those tiny spiders here. Armies of teeny spiders on the floor, walls, or maybe… the ceiling?

Panic prickled along her back, tingling across her shoulders, and she could not take a full breath. When she cautiously peeked directly above her, she saw a mass of spiders spreading across the ceiling, and she fainted.

Lucky

Lucky was so close to Brigit that he could smell the herbs giving her a constant and unique scent. Willowy in form, the simple fitted white dresses she always wore gave her an elegance that didn't match her cute snub nose. Born in the same era as him, the green in her eyes matched his, but hers were fringed with long lashes.

She was talking, and he tried to listen. "…a strange change in the High Court meetings I've been attending. They had become barely more than check-ins, but now? They are highly charged. People have not had such strong opinions in a hundred years or more."

Lucky nodded in sympathy at having to attend annoying meetings. He remembered the meetings he'd been forced to hold as king long ago. Those were bad enough, but the Tua

De court was filled with an arrogant master of each valued skill. Pretentious musicians, poets, historians, smiths, and more. As the oldest and best healer, Brigit was one of the lifetime members, never replaced.

Back when he was young, Lucky was accepted as qualified for any of the skilled master roles and still was for most of them these days. Although he was glad his newer duties as ham deliverer for MacLir kept him from being tempted to serve on the court.

Robin paced next to the pair, his youthful frenetic energy reminding Lucky of a bouncy puppy. Then, cutting Brigit off mid-sentence, Robin shouted, "Where could she be? Amy! AMY! Lucky, can you go check the other hallway?"

Ah, the urgency of youth. Lucky gave Brigit a knowing smile. She nodded, the curls in her dark brown hair bouncing. Lucky was briefly distracted by the memory of Brigit at a picnic long ago, remembering those same dark curls glinting gold in the sunlight. Pulling in a little more power to flash away, he disappeared from the hallway. Reappearing in a nearby parallel tunnel, he shouted, "Amy!"

With no reply, he checked one of the forks of the path he'd been on. "Amy!" Lucky shouted again. Still no response and no sign of the girl. She couldn't have gone far.

He reappeared next to Brigit, enjoying the whiff of herbs washing over him. After so many centuries using his power as the god of travelers, he was adept at landing precisely where he meant to. However, Brigit probably didn't know that, and he'd flashed in closer to her each time he returned.

Tilting her head, a smile playing across her lips, it was clear this time she noticed his proximity. Lucky stayed in her personal space a moment too long before gracefully retreating. Playing this game with her was fun, but he wished he were brave enough to hold her long elegant fingers in his. The dark cave would hide the hand-holding from Robin, not that the young man babbling at him would notice anything right now, not even a troll stampede.

Robin leaned forward. "Did you find her? We could hear you calling, but I didn't hear her answer."

"I didn't see or hear anything," Lucky replied, "but don't worry, we'll find her. She's here somewhere." His words were proven true on the next fork they tried.

"Amy!" shouted Robin, rushing to a girl on the ground.

Lucky's heart leaped into his throat at seeing Robin's friend collapsed. Wide-eyed, he peered through the dark at Brigit, who put one hand on Lucky's arm and her other hand on Robin's head. "CALM," she said. "The girl is okay, just sleeping."

Then he caught sight of the spiders. The creatures massed on the ceiling above the girl, crawling in circles or over each other in agitated movements. He'd never seen spiders in the tunnels. Usually, the magical wards kept bugs from getting in. He exchanged a worried glance with Brigit, then went to help Robin with the girl.

Amy

Amy woke, lying on something soft with sheer white gauzy curtains hanging around her. Robin came into view and helped her sit.

"You fainted from fear?" Robin asked.

"How did you know?" The question came out as a growled challenge. Apparently, fainting had brought back her angry mood.

"Brigit told me. She is good at understanding minds." A tall woman stood nearby. Her beautiful unreadable face was framed with silky dark brown hair. Ethereal green eyes marked her as one of them. A Tua De, like those who sneered at her and insulted Robin.

"Great. Another one. Robin, can we go back to the city? I don't want to stay here anymore." Amy dramatically fell back into the bed with an arm over her eyes. She could often tell when she was letting her temper run wild, but wasn't usually able to stop it.

"What is your problem?" Robin asked, his tone reproachful as he stood, distancing himself from her.

"My problem? What's your problem? You bring me to this horrible place, abandoning me alone in the tunnels, and then accuse me of having a problem?"

Brigit clapped loudly. "Enough," she said. "No squabbling over a misunderstanding. Robin, you apologize first."

"Unfair," he grumbled, his brows knitting in annoyance, but added, "I'm sorry our visit to the faerie mounds went sideways. I guess it's mostly my fault for leaving her alone. And I am sorry for yelling just now. But you were being mean to Brigit, my only friend growing up."

Amy internally groaned as she realized who this Tua De must be. She sat up again and apologized, first to Brigit and then to Robin, who patted her shoulder. "Let's go somewhere quiet to talk," he said.

Traveling a broader and cleaner hallway together, Amy told Robin the short story of her first and last spy mission. Glossing over the mean comments by the confrontational men, and completely leaving out the part about babies.

"Did you hear anything useful?" Robin asked.

"I don't know. I heard a few pieces of some sentences. They were talking about stone dolls?"

Robin shrugged and guided her around a corner to a door off the main hallway. He kept his arm around her as he opened it, but she halted, refusing to step inside.

The door confused her. "How does that work? You can't screw a door into the dirt. I've been to house building sites, and you can't have a door unless you build a door frame. It's impossible for that door to stand as it is."

The door fell, coming out of the crumbling dirt. Hinges and all.

"You broke my door!" said Robin, stunned.

"I didn't break it. The thing was architecturally impossible."

"Hmm. What if I told you the door frame was there, but hidden by dirt?"

"Is it?"

Robin only barely hesitated before saying, "Yes." He picked up the door and asked, "Can you picture the door frame?"

"I suppose I can see how it's possible to conceal it."

He brushed the soft dirt away to reveal a shiny hinge attached to bright new wood. He hooked the door to the board, mumbling, "Interesting."

Inside, a small single bed and dresser were the only pieces of furniture, along with a shelf attached to the back wall holding a few trinkets.

"This is where we'll stay tonight and where I grew up. Home sweet home," said Robin with a nervous chuckle.

"It's actually kinda cozy," Amy replied with a smile.

Robin patted the seat next to him on the bed. "I am sorry about earlier. Truly." She sat close and he tucked her hair behind an ear, saying with mock sincerity, "If you can't forgive me, I know a seal who wants to kiss you."

He grinned and Amy laughed remembering the flirty blue seal. "Don't worry, I'd rather kiss you."

When their eyes met, the laughter was sucked out of the room and replaced with an emotional charge Amy knew well from her days of exploring haylofts with farm boys. As she fell into his gaze, the green of soft new leaves in the spring, she barely heard him ask, "Can I kiss you?"

She grinned, tilting her head to show her agreement, not losing the intoxicating eye contact until his soft lips met hers.

CHAPTER 6

Amy

The next morning Amy opened her eyes to see the same soft ceiling glow that had been in some of the tunnels and Brigit's room. With no windows, it was difficult to tell what time it was. After an uncomfortable night on a bed meant for one, she was very ready to get back to the hotel today. As she pulled away from Robin's arms to stand and stretch she realized she needed a restroom before they left, but had no idea where it was located.

Shaking Robin's shoulder, Amy asked, "Where is the bathroom?"

"Corner," he mumbled sleepily.

The corner? Behind the footboard, she found a short vase with a wide mouth. "Oh no. No, no, definitely not. Just, no."

From behind her, Robin chuckled. "Yes." He leaned on his elbow, more awake now, giving her a great view of his bare chest.

"No," she said again. "I'm the kind of girl who needs plumbing. I refuse to empty my own, well, anything."

"That's the best part. The pot never fills."

"Explain."

"When you use it, the stuff disappears."

"Where does it go?"

"Nowhere."

"Since it existed, it cannot just un-exist. It must go somewhere."

"Try it and see."

Amy relieved herself on the chamber pot, sure it could not work. "See, it's still there," she said smugly.

Eyebrows furrowed and head tilted with uncertainty, Robin crawled across the bed. He put his hands on the footboard like a curious cat and peeked over into the pot to see a yellow puddle. "But," he protested, then stared at her, understanding dawning in his eyes. "Oh, now I remember," he said conversationally. "The chamber pot is hooked up to, um, a black hole deep in space. So, sometimes it takes a moment to empty."

"Oh. That's possible, I suppose? Magic, right? Oh, there it goes!"

Robin looked in time to see the bottom of the pot drop away to show a dark hole with a slight roaring sound, like listening to the ocean in a seashell. Intense cold crept into the warm room, and the chamber pot started to frost over with ice crystals.

"Does the bottom come back?" Amy asked, peering into the pot.

"Yes!" said Robin urgently.

She hoped that was true, and the bottom popped back into place with a click.

Robin's mouth dropped open. "I think we need to leave the mounds. Now."

"Why?"

"May not be safe."

"You've lived here for so long. What could be dangerous now?"

"You. You're a follower."

"A what?"

"It's what the faeries call them. Humans who have such a strong belief in their own thoughts that they can bend reality. Faeries recruit them as followers to help with ceremonies. You are the most powerful I've ever seen. Or even heard of." He scrambled around for his clothes and said, "Do me a favor and only think about… flowers. How harmful could that be?"

"Where are the flowers?"

"Anywhere you want them to be," he said absently, tying his shoes.

"Some violets along the tunnels would make them more cheerful. And sunflowers."

Robin shouldered his pack, opened the door, and froze. Amy pushed him forward and followed him out into the tunnel to see violets in a row along the hall with a sunflower on either side of every door.

"But how?" she asked.

Robin grabbed her hand and dashed past the flowers, then raced around a couple of corners and two connecting busy kitchens. In the third kitchen, they plunged straight into the wall. Through dirt first, then roots and grass, until sunlight fell on Amy's face and arms. Robin collapsed on the soft green ground and pulled out a phone.

"MacLir, we're outside the faerie kitchens and a little stranded. Could you pick us up?"

Piper

This was it. The moment she hoped would happen. She was going to meet the follower with the most power anyone had seen in a very long time. It's what Robin said in her vision, and she hoped it was true.

Piper changed into her faerie dress and braided her hair into a crown. Best to create a good impression of goddesses in general, considering she wanted the girl to become one too. MacLir called her name from the deck, so they must be close. She put the last few pins in her braid and picked up Flutter.

"We are about to meet someone, and I need you to act amazing."

"I don't need to act. I am amazing." The kitten pumped her wings, lifting off Piper's hands to land on her shoulder.

"Stop nibbling on my hair. I just got it perfect. I need her to know you are not an ordinary human world cat."

"My wings might give her a clue." Flutter gave Piper's ear a final lick, then flopped down, her back legs resting on Piper's shoulder blade and her front claws gripping the dress.

Piper rolled her eyes, but scanned the room one more time, wondering if there was anything else she could do to look more impressive. She caught sight of the daisies MacLir had brought her. She pulled three of them from the vase, snipped off most of the stem, and wove them into her braid. Perfect.

She considered finding her shoes, but that seemed a bit too much. Padding barefoot out of the room, she focused on not tripping through the green room, down the short hall, and onto the deck. Her timing was excellent.

Robin was helping the girl climb over the edge of the ship, so Piper got to see her amazement as she took in Wave Sweeper. The beautiful polished wood grain, billowy glimmering sails in blue and green, emeralds and sapphires lining the ship's rim, the dragon figurehead, and soon, the two magical beings who lived here.

Robin clasped the girl's hand and said, "This is Amy."

"Hello, welcome! I'm MacLir, god of the sea." He was wearing only brown cloth pants with laces up the sides. Piper smiled, pleased MacLir wore her favorite of his pants today. He must have also remembered she'd asked him to show off because he added, "I can control saltwater. And talk to sea creatures."

"Do you talk to animals a lot?" Amy asked with a kind smile. Piper liked her. She didn't often feel comfortable around people right away. Still, this first impression gave her hope for a relationship with Amy.

"Surprisingly, they don't have much to say to me," replied MacLir. "Although, animals have a lot to say to Piper." He waved a hand in her direction, where she was still standing, partly hidden in the cabin's doorway.

Piper braced herself. This was her moment. She'd decided on airy for her character role, confident she could pull off that act for this short meeting. She twirled out of the doorway, doing a spin that flared her blue dress, the glittering bits twinkling as they caught the sunlight.

"Your turn," she sent to Flutter, "do something charming." She pushed the thought into Flutter's mind and the cat, perhaps sensing her desperation, for once agreed to do as she asked. The kitten launched from her shoulder, silvery wings coasting on the ocean breeze toward Amy. Landing gracefully at her feet, Flutter nuzzled Amy's leg, audibly purring.

When Amy looked up again, Piper held MacLir's hand—showing Piper belonged in this world—and said, "Hello Amy, I'm the goddess of love and matchmaking." She was pleased with her confident tone. Maybe she was settling into this new life after all. MacLir grinned down at her and squeezed her hand gently to show he'd noticed her odd behavior. She glanced a smile at him, then focused on the couple in front of her.

"Piper is the reason we're together," added Robin. "The goddess knew we'd fall in love, so she sent me to the airport to meet ya."

Piper was confused by the expression crossing Amy's face. Was she happy? Upset? MacLir lifted Piper off her feet, saying, "Ah, so that's what this was all about." Piper tried to connect the bits of conversation, but MacLir distracted her with a cheerful kiss. She kissed him back, hiding her confusion as he sat them on one side of the bench.

"I keep thinking about lengthening this bench, but it's so cozy as it is, right?" MacLir laughed. It was the friendly contagious laugh Piper loved so much, and she smiled at how well this was going when the others laughed too.

Amy and Robin squished onto the other bench, also in a seat meant for one. They shared a shy smile as they twined their fingers together. "Very cozy," agreed Robin. "Finally, a match from Piper that worked. She's tried to pair me with a stray cat and a rescue dog from the faerie mounds, but I'm not at home enough to care for either, so I declined."

"I would too," said Amy with a shudder. "I'd decline being in charge of any living thing."

"Even a baby?" asked Piper.

"Especially a baby."

Dismayed, Piper ignored Robin and MacLir's chatting as she focused on a reading to check Amy's love life. It still showed the meeting at the airport and, more importantly, still showed a baby. Again, Piper was reassured, but confused. In the vision, Amy wasn't any older than she appeared now, so a baby could happen soon. Piper thought Amy would want to get pregnant based on the baby that she saw in the vision, but what if she actually didn't?

"So, you two, what happened?" asked MacLir. "You said you were stranded, but we found you outside the kitchens. That's one of the entrances any Tua De can use without my help."

"We couldn't go back through the Otherworld to get home because Amy was destroying it."

"I only believed what you told me!" Amy said, her eyes narrowed at Robin.

"She's a follower," he explained with a shrug.

"I'm not anyone's follower," she grumbled, but remained silent through Robin's story. Starting with how she'd believed into being an army of spiders, then both a door frame and rows of flowers, on top of connecting the chamber pot to somewhere unknown. When he finished, she complained, "I don't understand the flowers, but Robin told me there was a door frame. And a black hole."

"Only so you could fix them. And I didn't think you'd be strong enough to actually connect to space."

Flutter curled in Piper's lap, and she pet the cat on autopilot while she considered Robin's story. This was better than she'd dreamed. Piper had not lived in the magic community long, but knew enough about followers to grasp how extraordinary Amy's power was. Amy was exactly what she needed, and it might not be possible to find this type of human again. Especially one already entwined in the magical community. Although, technically, getting Amy pulled into the magical world had been her doing.

Piper's only worry was how Amy didn't seem likely to agree to have a child. The toddler she'd seen in her visions was only one possibility. If Amy didn't want a baby it would be wrong to force her into it, and yet, it felt like everything hinged on Amy's baby. Piper needed more time to convince her.

MacLir ran a hand through his spiked blond hair and said, "I've seen this strength before. However, not for a long time. Amy has a sturdy mind. In the human world, she would be called headstrong, maybe stubborn. The Otherworld is more flexible, full of potential, so she can mold the world around her. It's all about belief versus reality. She did not believe a door could stand on its own, however, she could believe your logical explanation. So, it became her reality." MacLir glanced sideways at Piper, adding, "Such power. You know, you could be amazing as a goddess of—ow!" MacLir abruptly yelped as Piper stood on his foot.

"How clumsy of me," she said, unsympathetic. The kitten, dumped out of her lap when she stood with no warning, was also annoyed. Flutter stalked into the cabin, tail lashing.

A plan began to form in Piper's head. To get the ball rolling, she said, "MacLir, weren't you saying earlier how you planned to give Robin a new task? He needs to find out where Ian is from."

"I was planning to talk to him about it later, but yes, that's true."

"It would require a lot of travel from Robin. You wouldn't want to split up Robin and Amy just as they found each other." An adventure would provide ample time to understand Amy better and find a way to talk to her about what Piper wanted. "So," continued Piper, her airy tone back, "we can all research Ian's past together. I could fly them around to the outer mounds, and they could keep me company since you're planning to go searching for Pig again soon."

"True…" MacLir said again. His forehead wrinkled as he inspected Piper's face for clues of her intentions.

"You are away so much, following leads and rumors about Pig or simply being distracted by the ocean. I get lonely. One day, with a baby, I'd have a tiny sidekick. In the meantime, I can take on human companions. Like Lucky used to."

"You have Flutter," MacLir pointed out.

"It's not the same," said Piper wistfully.

MacLir pulled her into a tight hug and whispered directly in her ear, "I think I know what you are doing, and it might work. Good luck."

He shed his long pants revealing black swim shorts underneath, and with a wave, he dived into the water.

CHAPTER 7

Amy

Amy lounged in the comfy bed, lazing amid the plush blankets and pillows, admiring the constellations in blue gemstones embedded in the ceiling. The ship, Wave Sweeper, was amazing. She was pleasantly surprised when she'd been shown the room and bathroom that would be her next accommodation on this amazing journey. Even more shocking, the ship didn't sail away from the dock, but instead lifted in the air.

The people living in it were odd, but kindred spirits. MacLir had not returned yet, but she liked him a lot from the one time they'd met. She was warming to Piper, especially after learning she was autistic. Everyone was different, but a few of Piper's quirks reminded Amy of Clara, her autistic older sister.

Making a friend of Piper was great, but the time with Robin was even better. After weeks of living on the ship with Robin, she felt they'd always been together and could not imagine a time in the future when they might have to part. She still wanted to experience her daydreams of travel to far-flung places, but now imagined those travels with Robin by her side. Robin was hesitant to leave Ireland, but even though he had his own bed in a green room that was a twin of her own, he often snuck into her room to chat. They'd spent multiple nights cuddled in the soft blue bed, staying up late talking about sightseeing trips around the world.

She prepared for the day and joined Piper out on the bench. The salty breeze was a welcome change from the dusty desert air of her childhood home. Piper was still watching the waves crash on the shore below, so lost in thought the goddess didn't notice her arrival. Amy scuffed her shoes, a slight noise that she used at home to let Clara know she was around, without startling her sister. It worked the same for Piper, who glanced over and smiled as a hello.

She returned her gaze to the sea, saying, "You know I've been doing some research since I came to live with MacLir. Because he's not even close to being human, we can't have children without magical intervention."

Amy didn't know what to say, so she settled nearby, listening instead of answering. Piper's pause was short, but she continued. "The most powerful would be if a goddess of motherhood granted our request for a child, but one does not exist in the world right now."

"Hard to tell with immortals, but you seem quite young. Having a baby can hardly be urgent, right?"

"True, I'm only 18 in human years, but it's what I want, so I'm determined."

"Are you sure you want children? They are noisy and sticky. All of my sisters have kids, but my autistic sister struggled with her two."

Piper shrugged, repeating, "I'm determined."

"Hello!" called Robin from below. "Spy returning!" he added as he clambered over the edge.

"Say it louder. I'm not sure everyone on the island heard you," said Amy with a flirty laugh. Robin was definitely terrible as a spy, but he tried hard. "Any luck with this mound?"

"No one knew Ian before a few weeks ago. Where could he have appeared from?"

"Have you learned anything from this visit?" asked Piper.

"Ian always wears a hat and won't take it off."

"That's… odd. But not useful."

"No, I guess not." Robin sighed. "We have one more place to check, and then I'm out of ideas."

Amy tried to hide her dismay. If there was nowhere else to search, the adventure would be over. They'd have to leave the ship, and she'd return to the hotel or Spain, or worse, return home. She might never see Robin again unless he agreed to leave Ireland with her. Deciding to make the most of the time left, she took Robin's hand, asking, "Can I go in with you? To the last place?"

Robin's eyes crinkled as some of the tension left his shoulders. "I would like that," he said, reaching for her hand and giving it a squeeze. "It will only be a short visit, do you think you can control your power while we are in the mounds?"

Amy's stomach twisted, remembering the spiders, but nodded. "I'll try."

When they arrived, Amy compared this place to the first faerie mound she'd seen. The great hall, the infirmary, and the kitchens were pristine and well-lit despite being underground in a muddy cave. However, this mound was truly filthy and gloomy. Ratty curtains hung over long ropes to separate the space into rooms only added to the shabby appearance.

"Hello!" called Robin. "Is anyone here?"

Robin pulled aside a curtain for Amy, and she stepped through, worried her shoes would never recover from this trip.

"Alright there?" A boy ducked around a curtain to their left, his clothes as threadbare as the fabric he stood near. It was hard to tell in the half-light, but he didn't appear much older than Amy.

"Hi," Robin greeted him. "I'm here to speak with your clan leader."

"He's legged it, but ya can speak to my ma. Come on."

Another boy appeared behind him, and the two led them to a stout woman. She was packing a small bag, flicked her gaze at them, and then continued her task.

"Your son said the clan leader is gone at the moment. Would you mind if I asked you a few questions?"

"Aye, if ye must."

"We're seeking the home of a Tua De named Ian."

"That man. Naw, he's not from our clan. He came touring through here like he owns the place. Spoutin' wild accusations no one should believe."

"I've heard some of his ideas. I can't say I believe any of them," agreed Robin.

"He won't find support under this roof either. My man was a human. He's long since passed, but the twins grow into him more every day."

The boys had stayed near their mother, leaning against the cave wall. "So, where is everyone?" asked Robin with a glance at the boys.

"Scarpered off. To join the cause," said the woman. "Awful thick, the lot o' them."

"Joining Ian?"

"Aye, what a mess. But we're shot of this manky place. Headed above ground. The boys want to live in the mortal world, and I'm going with them. Hang the rules, I say."

Robin backed away, preparing to leave, but Amy held him in place through their linked hands. "One more question," she said, "before we go. If you could tell us anything you know about Ian, we'd appreciate it. Anything unusual he said while he was here?"

"The boys might know sommit. They was spinning a tall tale to anyone what would listen." She nodded toward them, giving them permission to speak to the strangers.

"Saw him arrive, didn't we?" said one boy to the other.

"He was not lookin' so polished as this last time he swept through the place."

"Aye, the gobshite was in rough shape. That great big sea dragon dumped him on the shore. Wearin' all white and shattered tired."

"He lay there forever, then come staggering through the easy entrance."

Robin thanked them and tugged Amy back to the cave opening they'd come through. The same entrance the boys had called easy. It had been explained to her how MacLir had made many of the entrances into the Otherworld, but he'd used places already weakened and thin. Some more than others were so weak even a human could accidentally stumble through them.

When they were a distance away, and the ship was in sight down the beach, Amy commented, "She sounded more Irish than anyone I've met here."

"This outpost must have spent a lot of time in the human world to gain a modern accent. The Tua De are not from Ireland, and I was raised by some of the oldest of them, so none of us sound the same as Irish speakers of this era."

Amy wondered how exhausting it would be to live through various eras of history. Would all that time crush a person under the weight of memories? Or would it be fun to watch history happen? Fun, she decided, but only as long as she was in a comfortable living situation. She remembered the sectioned-off cave the boys and their mother lived in and compared that with the tiny room Robin grew up in. Neither was appealing. "Do all the Tua De live in such poverty?"

"More often than I'd like. The mounds are getting crowded. When they first came underground, they could all fit in the main mound. Now, though… with so many split-off clans, it's lucky if you can find a clean place to sleep. I was lucky to have Brigit watching over me."

Piper

Piper waited on the beach while sitting on a piece of drift-wood, with the ship parked behind her. Watching the waves again, wishing MacLir was here. Wishing MacLir's child was in her arms.

Flutter glided from the top of the cabin and sat on the log next to her. "Hey. See that gull? It's smaller than the others. Think I could take it in a fight?"

"No," Piper replied, not taking her eyes off the waves.

"MacLir always brings me those little crunchy fishes. Do you think he'll be back soon?"

"No," she said again, the wistful tone in her own voice surprising her. MacLir was so often gone, although she hoped that would happen less after the pig was found.

"If I can't eat the gull or the crunchy fish, can I have some tuna?" Flutter asked hopefully.

"Definitely not. I don't have a spare room to put you in for the rest of the day and I don't want you stinking up my room."

Flutter's huff of annoyance was less in Piper's mind and more in the way the cat's shoulders stiffened as she hunched, tail flicking in swift jerks.

Piper shook her head at the kitten's antics, but she was cheered. Watching the waves with Flutter nearby helped her loneliness in MacLir's absence. Besides, animals always made her happier, sitting with them or simply observing them. For several minutes, Piper had kept an eye on motion in the waves, wondering what animal it could be, until she realized it was a set of eyes. Watching her. Fia.

The sea dragon rose from the waves when spotted and moved as close as the water would let her. "Hello, friend," Fia said. Their tone was cheerful, but the dragon glanced both ways and tensed as if expecting an attack.

It occurred to Piper she couldn't hear Fia's thoughts. She

could almost assume her ability to communicate with animals was faulty, or maybe it didn't apply to the animal who gave her the gift. However, with MacLir not being able to read Fia as a sea creature… it made Piper curious about what the dragon really was. "Hi, Fia. What are you up to today?"

"Oh, this and this. That and that," replied the dragon airily, still swinging their head back and forth to scan the beach.

"Are you waiting for someone here?" Piper asked, peering around and pulling Flutter closer, just in case.

"No. Yes. And No."

"Can I help you with something?"

"Not today." Fia ducked back into the waves as two figures approached.

Piper almost didn't recognize her shipmates with the sun to their backs, but called to Fia, "It's okay. I know these two. You can come back out."

Ears poked out of the water first, followed by the dragon's eyes as their ears laid back flat like a wary cat. Piper waved to come back, so the dragon did, but slowly.

"Actually, we need to talk to you, Fia," called Robin. "What do you know about a Tua De named Ian?"

"I don't keep track of names," said Fia, dismissively.

"He's a large fellow. Some kids say he was on this beach with you. He was dressed all in white."

"Lots of people wear white." Fia's mouth opened and closed as if wanting to say more. Their long fangs on display made Amy take a few steps back.

Robin held his ground. "True, but do you talk to all of them?"

"No," Fia answered this one question firmly.

"Do you remember talking to someone on the beach or bringing a man to this beach?"

At Robin's demanding tone, Fia's scales rippled. The blue and green discs caught the light as they lifted and clacked back in place. "I, um… I have come to this beach before, before… before today." The dragon seemed increasingly distressed, lizard-like eyes darting wildly.

"Was there a man here? Can you tell us anything about him?"

The dragon's tail lashed the water. Creating more foam than the waves. "I, I… a man, men sometimes, men are…"

Glancing reproachfully at Robin, Piper stood and said, "It's okay, Fia. If it upsets you, you don't have to say anything."

The sea dragon focused on Piper a moment, then dropped straight into the waves, disappearing from sight.

Ian

"Can I take your hat, sir?" asked the butler, his white-gloved hand outstretched.

"No. It's mine," replied Ian, grabbing the edges and pulling it on tighter to prove his point.

When the man left, Ian's fingers explored the edges of the hat for any visible hair. Worried as always. If even a stray hair came out from under it… the thought made him sweat.

Waiting by the door, he examined the opulence the High Court member lived in. Unless he knew for sure, he'd never be able to tell this was an underground cave. A house had been built with the front door perfectly lined up to the cave's entrance.

A grand staircase curved up from the entryway, above the only other door on the ground floor, the office door the butler had disappeared into. Ian could almost see doors upstairs, probably bedrooms. High ceilings with chandeliers flooded the gold-gilded room with light. Light even shined through and around the curtained windows. He peeked behind the curtains of one and found bright heat lamps creating the deception of sun-soaked windows. A non-magic illusion, but a good one.

He contrasted this with the squalor he'd seen recently while visiting the clan mounds. People were living in actual mud. Tuatha Dé Danann living in mud? It could not be borne. This was the change he needed to bring about. All of them should band together again, then one day soon, they would all live similar to the owner of this house. This cave-not-cave was even better than the place he was raised.

The butler returned, cutting his musings short. He followed the servant into the office under the stairs, stunned at its size. So much larger than he expected from the outside. The study was lined with books and scattered with heavy furniture. A man stood from the massive desk, skeletal thin, in a perfectly fitting business suit.

He waved Ian toward a pair of chairs, and the High Court member sat opposite him asking, "How is the recruitment?"

"Finished. I've visited every clan and stripped them of as many people as would come with us."

Rumors said this man ran questionable businesses in the mortal world. With his crow-like hungry eyes, Ian could believe it. He was glad to find such an impressive ally, even if the man did make him feel short.

Ian pulled in power, an action so much easier to do here in Ireland, and in his most honeyed voice said, "I'm glad you're my ally. And you are glad you're my ally."

The High Court member's eyes unfocused, and he repeated what Ian said. Ian worried he'd laid it on too thick. He needed the man to trust him, not be completely witless. "I'm here to discuss troops," he reminded the man, without a trace of power in his voice.

The man shook himself. "Right. The troops. We've rented a hotel in the mortal world and have them all there. It's better than anything they've seen before, and many have not been to the human world in a long time. Being warm, clean, and fed with room service means they are showing quite a lot of loyalty at the moment."

"Excellent." Ian clapped his hands. "Since we are set for troops, what about the applications for more inner circle members?"

"They have all been approved, except for one."

"Robin?"

The High Court member shuffled through some papers, searching for one. "Yes. Everyone still finds it suspicious that he has lived among humans. However, an inner circle member is vouching for him. So, we are in a disagreement on moving forward."

Ian mulled over the options. Either Robin was a real recruit, or an inner circle member was a traitor. Then, adding only a touch of power to his voice, Ian commanded, "Keep an eye on him and inform me of any developments."

"Yes, sir," the powerful court member replied. The slight crease in his forehead was the only indication he was used to hearing those words rather than saying them.

CHAPTER
8

Piper

"How is my little sister?" Clara asked to welcome Amy through the front door and into the entryway. Clara's mass of messy shoulder-length brown curls bouncing with enthusiasm, causing her whole body to bob in place. Amy rushed to give the older woman a hug, and something Clara said caused a startled laugh to burst from Amy as she swatted her sister's hand away from her hair.

Piper watched the exchange with interest. As an only child, this easy banter was something she only ever shared with MacLir. She'd thought it was part of love, although sisters loved each other, so it made sense.

Actually, love is weird, Piper decided. You can apparently love everything from people to shiny rocks. Or, in her case, simply be fascinated with people and shiny rocks. She was still having trouble telling the difference. Was she only enchanted with the idea of love for MacLir? Perhaps at first, but by now, it must be love. Or, something like it, an understanding of each other that would continue to grow over time.

And having a baby? She knew herself well enough to know it was another idea she was becoming absorbed by.

Although, perhaps it would be another fascination that would lead to love. She was sure of it. Still refusing to give up, Piper knew she'd find a way to have what she wanted. If not with Amy today, then someone else tomorrow. One day, she'd have MacLir's baby.

In the meantime, Amy was still her best chance. So, when her new friend asked if it was possible for Piper to fly her and Robin to visit with her sister, Piper happily agreed, and MacLir returned from his most recent Pig search in time to join them. She had not found a good way to bring up what she wanted from Amy, so now might be the best way to gather insight into what might make Amy agree. Except that meant she was at an unfamiliar house, caught in this family visit. She wished her obsessions didn't push her into uncharted territory so often.

Robin crowded behind Amy, so Piper stepped out of the way behind MacLir. Waiting in a line to meet people was its own kind of agony. She would be happiest if she was introduced last. Or never.

Clara's welcome to her sister had been warm and chipper, but she became reserved as she met Robin. Piper watched her go from happy to formal in an instant. Having worn enough masks, she could recognize the transition in others. Clara leaned slightly away as she gave him a wave, and Piper decided to remember that trick later to fend off future unwanted welcome hugs or handshakes.

Hoping to reassure Clara, Piper did what she wished others would do when meeting her or anyone. First, she mimicked Clara's wave—instead of offering a handshake or a hug—then smiled and gave a single head nod, almost a bow, keeping her eyes downcast.

It seemed to work, as Clara's voice had softened when she said, "Nice to meet you, welcome to my home."

Piper had been bracing for this moment since the trip was

discussed. She hated going into other people's homes. The smell usually hit first. If it wasn't overwhelmingly human, it was overpoweringly chemical. She never knew where to sit or where to put her hands. Unbearable if people expected her to eat something messy in front of them.

Her worries were eased when Clara led them straight through a clean kitchen to an open-air patio. The table had exactly enough chairs for everyone, would hide her hands, and held a platter full of prepackaged bite-size snacks. Piper relaxed into a chair between MacLir and Amy, and peace settled over her. Maybe this trip would not be so bad after all.

Clara shooed the men off to gather drinks from the kitchen. Without any classic small talk, she started the conversation by saying, "So, Amy tells me you're autistic."

"She says the same about you," replied Piper, with a shy smile.

"That's better than most of the things people say about me." The twinkle in Clara's brown eyes was back, and her lips twisted in an impish grin.

Somehow, this woman reminded Piper of her favorite aunt. The one person who believed in her when she was growing up. They looked completely different, though. Clara's skin was darker, her mess of bouncy curls nothing like her aunt's straight thin layers. Yet, her friendly squinty eyes eased Piper's tension.

In Piper's thoughtful silence, Clara continued the conversation.

"I would tell you about my day, but it was frustrating before you all arrived, so I won't annoy you with it." Clara's hands waved wildly as she said rapidly, "It's the most awful ordeal when people you barely know ramble on about a bad day. Sometimes, I wish people had a mute button. I often have nothing to say at the end of their tirade except, 'That sounds annoying.' Because honestly, I usually don't know if it is annoying or not, but you have to say something, right?"

"Right," agreed Piper, still trying to process Clara's rushed chatter. "The phrase, 'That sounds annoying,' is a good one. I'll try to remember it. 'That's rough' is all I have for people sharing their problems."

Clara threw her arms wide, saying, "Good gravy! People complain at me so much I've typed a whole list of ways to commiserate and show sympathy."

"Ooo, could you send it to me?" Piper loved the idea of a list of ready phrases. She quickly mentally listed all the different lists she could create around this new idea.

Amy, who had kept silent, watching her sister and new friend, rolled her eyes and commented, "When two autistics meet and compare notes on scripting."

"Roll your eyes at us again, and I'll sneak spinach into your dinner. Scripting is important. We survive in a world not designed for us. We must have words ready, because at any moment, an unknown person might insist they put their sweaty palm against your clean fingers for a handshake. Or a neighbor might invite you to their annual barbecue party. Again."

Both Piper and Clara shuddered at the horrific notion while Amy laughed and asked, "What's wrong with a barbecue?"

Piper and Clara made brief eye contact and nodded to each other. It seemed they both agreed about dreaded parties, but neither would bother explaining it to someone who could never understand.

The reasons Piper had never accepted an invitation by someone she barely knew were the same reasons she almost didn't attend today's event. She could have flown Amy and Robin to this house and simply stayed on the ship. Actually, she'd desperately wanted to do just that, but there was a specific reason she'd agreed to come inside.

Since Piper felt like she'd made an instant friend, something that had only ever happened with MacLir, she got straight to the point of her reasons for being here. Focusing her eyes on Clara, ignoring Amy in her periphery, Piper announced, "I need information about your stubborn sister."

Clara snorted. "I have many stubborn sisters. We come from a long line of strong-willed women. But I assume you mean Amy."

"Yes. Amy. I need to know how to get her to accept... becoming a goddess."

Amy

Amy inwardly groaned. She didn't know what Piper was getting at with the sudden goddess talk, but she had not figured out a good way to tell Clara about magic yet. She wasn't ready for her usually practical sister to think she'd tangled with crazy people. In fact, if she could have hidden it forever, that would be ideal.

"Amy? A goddess?" Clara asked, her head tilted as she flicked her eyes to Amy, then back to Piper.

MacLir returned, setting cold bottles on the table, followed by Robin with a water pitcher. "Oh, yes," agreed MacLir, "she could be an amazing goddess."

Amy thought back through the weeks aboard Wave Sweeper and could not remember a single time Piper had mentioned anything about this. Her mind whirled with the idea that she could have magic like Piper's, but her sister asked what they meant before she could.

"What would you be a goddess of? Perhaps the Perky Goddess of Perfectly Plucked Eyebrows?" Clara raised and lowered her own eyebrows, her mischievous grin back. "Or... let's see, how about the Goddess of Anxiety? Goddess of Fainting? Something more tangible... how about Goddess of all the Horses? Goddess of Stables? Oh! I've got it! Goddess of… the Hayloft!" Clara elbowed Amy as she returned to raising and lowering her eyebrows.

Robin narrowed his eyes, and Amy blushed, announcing, "New subject." Her sister was taking this well, unless she didn't actually believe them. Hopefully, Amy could keep it that way, but Clara would not let it go.

"No wait, I'm intrigued. What would she be a goddess of?" Clara asked with a chuckle.

Piper turned to Amy, desire shining in her eyes, and Amy realized she might have a problem. Piper only had this look in her eye when she was talking about babies, but what would that have to do with Amy? In a single word from Piper, Amy's stomach dropped. "Fertility."

Clara, who did not hear the hope in Piper's one-word answer, burst out laughing. Between cackles, she managed to gasp out, "Fertility? Amy?" The older woman laughed so hard she snorted, making her laugh harder. "Amy's always ranted against pregnancy and motherhood! What a good joke! Unless…" she stopped laughing as she soaked in the gravity of the atmosphere around the table. She propped her chin on her fist looking between all of them. "Good gravy! Y'all are serious about this."

Amy finally found her voice to ask, "Me? You want me to become a goddess of babies? I see the longing in your eyes when you talk about children, and my chest hurts for your pain, but I don't think I could do that."

Piper's eyes brimmed with tears, and MacLir put his arm around her.

"Maybe if I knew more about the power," Amy said in a rush. "About what it could do?"

Having magic might be fantastic. Calling herself goddess sounded good too. It didn't seem likely, but it would be wonderful if someone would say something to change her mind.

MacLir finally broke the silence. "As I understand it, from Brigit's explanation, it would be similar to Piper's power of matchmaking. The future has many possibilities depending on the choices people make. Piper's power allows her to see into the future of if-she-intervenes. If she does not nudge that first meeting of two people who would fall in love, the future will take a different path than what she saw. Right?"

"Right," agreed Piper.

"So, based on that, Amy would also be able to see into the future paths of if-she-intervenes to make anyone pregnant, or not. You could see if it's a good time for the mother or if she will even be a good mother. Then, you can choose. To intervene, you simply believe it will happen. Your mind is strong. The vision will be a waking dream, you will have watched it happen, so it should be easy to believe in. If you don't want the woman to become pregnant, it should be easy also. If you don't want to believe, then a different future will happen."

Amy's mind spun. MacLir had never said so much at once or so seriously. She braced herself to upset Piper by refusing again, but mulling it over, she had an idea.

"Does it have to be the goddess of babies, or fertility, or whatever? Piper once told me that fertility is only one aspect of Brigit's power. Could I be a goddess of something else? And still help Piper?"

MacLir hesitated, then finally answered, "That would be a good question for Brigit. She knows a lot more about it, but with a mind like yours, I suppose it's possible you could be a goddess with multiple powers."

Robin sat up straighter, and his eyes lit up. "I know what to say to make you want it!" he declared triumphantly.

Amy grinned at his tone. "Oh, really?"

"Yes! I know you, Amy Perez. Ready?"

Amy nodded.

"MacLir, you said Amy can choose if any woman becomes pregnant, or not, with her power. Right?"

MacLir hesitated, considering Robin's words before saying, "Yes. Correct."

Robin twisted back to Amy, his body language shouting smugness. "No birth control is a hundred percent effective. Amy, if you were to go through the ceremony to gain the power MacLir was talking about, you would be your own birth control! You could make sure you never ever get pregnant."

Amy only had to think about it for the briefest of moments. She slapped her hand hard on the table, startling both Clara and Piper, and shouted, "Yes! I want in. This might work."

CHAPTER 9

Lucky

Lucky stood outside Brigit's door. Staring at it. Willing himself to go inside. "I'm on my way to lunch. Would you eat some lunch with me?" he mumbled to himself. "Or, I'd love for you to join me for lunch. No. Would you like to join me for lunch?" The last one sounded okay, and it gave him the courage to grasp the door handle.

The door was pulled from the other side as he did, and he lurched forward, bumping into Brigit.

She caught his hand to steady to him. "Oh! Lucky. What are you… I mean, I was going to get lunch… but are you ill? I can stay if you need me."

His practice sentences didn't fit anything she'd said. "I'm going to lunch too," he finally replied.

"Here in the infirmary?" she asked, eyes sparkling with a mischievous smile. He realized she must have checked him for injuries by now and discovered his only distress was emotional.

"No." Lucky pulled himself together, trying to ignore how distracting her palm felt against his. "I came to ask you out to lunch."

The smile played on her lips as she tilted her head. "Ask me… out?"

"For lunch," Lucky agreed.

"I accept. Where are we going?" She took a firmer grip of his hand and shut the door behind her to walk with him out of the mounds.

"A great little place over in Sweden I hope you'll like. I'm borrowing MacLir's ship today."

Sitting across from Brigit on the L-shaped mast bench, they lapsed into a tension-filled silence. He wished he could chat like MacLir was able to do while flying. However, making the ship obey him took all his concentration. When they got close enough, he dropped the ship gracefully onto the still surface of the ocean, and it steadily moved forward through the water, slicing the waves into a traditional ship's wake toward the harbor.

Strolling along the street together to the cafe, quiet happiness overtook Lucky as warmth spread through him. Mostly he didn't admit it, but he was also as lonely as he could tell Piper was most days, with MacLir out on the hunt for his pig. It was difficult to find a kindred spirit he felt comfortable around in this world moving too fast for him and changing too much. Yet, he still could not pinpoint why he was so attracted to Brigit these days.

The silence stretched, but he didn't interrupt her first view of the fishing village since she said nothing either. White-walled, red-roofed houses lined the hilly lane they walked, and a whiff of processing dead fish breezed through the whole district. Wispy white clouds hovered overhead, the blue sky lying about how chilly the wind was.

The cafe was bustling with locals and tourists, but they soon found a corner table with an ocean view. After eating lunch over small talk, Lucky was finally ready to start a real conversation, but realized he had nothing to say. Searching for something to begin with, he said, "So, we'll have a new king soon." He immediately regretted bringing up politics. Nothing was less romantic.

"I miss the old kings," said Brigit, wistfully. Then her expression shifted to anger, face flushed with a tinge of red. "I've lived a whole human lifespan above ground and three more underground. It wasn't so bad at first, but the way the Tua De live now? It's degrading. We're a pale imitation of once-great people, rulers and kings every one of us. Reduced to squalor."

Lucky didn't know what to say. He wished he'd picked any other topic. "I didn't know you were so passionate about it."

"Otherworld time seems to stand still. The mortal world has passed three thousand years. We have passed barely three hundred. They may have forgotten what they did, but we still remember. After the war, you spent a lot of time in the Otherworld, so you don't have many first-hand memories of our true golden age. When the High Court ruled Ireland and humans had to obey us."

Lucky frowned slightly. It almost sounded like Voiceless Pure talk, but not quite. Maybe she was only being nostalgic? He was about to ask her for clarification, when Odin arrived at the cafe.

The Scandinavian god of war and magic was dressed wholly in shades of gray. Medium gray shirt, pants, heavy boots, shaggy silvery gray beard, dark gray eye patch, weathered gray wooden staff, and long-ish gray fuzzy hair topped with a felted pointy hat. The hat, slumped over from too much rain and not enough shaping, was also gray.

Brigit greeted him warmly with a simple happy, "Hello," and Lucky asked, "Want to get some dessert with us? My treat!"

"Happy to." Odin's voice was a deep growl, not unpleasant, but as weathered as the rest of him. As the server, an energetic young girl, popped over to take their lunch plates, he added, "The waffles in this place are very good." Taking his recommendation, Brigit ordered a waffle with strawberry jam and whipped cream. Lucky got vanilla ice cream with hot fudge on his. Odin ordered a plain waffle to eat with a drizzle of honey.

Odin began catching up on gossip with Brigit, so Lucky's mind drifted. He idly watched the cheerful server at her work. Hurrying from one customer to the next, ensuring everyone had napkins or delivering food. Her red hair in braids, freckles on any exposed skin, and her short dress swishing with every quick maneuver. She smiled the whole time, even winning over potentially irate customers waiting too long or with a not-quite-right order.

He sensed her mood was focused, and she was trying to ignore how much her feet hurt. He realized he was staring and shifted his attention to his tablemates as she headed in their direction with the tab. She hesitated, not sure who to hand the check to, and smiled broadly at Lucky when he rescued her by reaching for it. "Thank you, sir. I'll be back shortly," she said.

"No need," said Lucky and handed the paper right back with the stack of bills in the local currency. As the server left, warmth spread from his hands to his toes and made him lightheaded. Then his skin started glowing faintly gold.

Lucky grinned at Brigit's surprised laugh, and Odin rolled his eyes into his bushy eyebrows. "Ha! I love when this happens," said Lucky quietly, as the glow mostly faded. He patted his pockets, searching for the pouch he knew must have appeared, finding it in time for the server to return. With one hand, Lucky snatched her delicate wrist. She tried to yank her hand away, but Lucky kept a good hold. The girl stared deeply into his eyes, getting lost in the sea of green, and she relaxed as his powers took hold.

Lucky, his skin still maintaining a golden sheen, delicately flipped her hand over, placing the pouch firmly in her palm and curling her fingers around it. "This is for you. For your hard work and belief in the old ways." She needed to know this was her gift from a god. He finally released her to stand and gallantly bowed. Motioning his two companions to follow, they all left without another word.

Immensely pleased with the day, he sauntered along the lane toward the marina, one elbow linked with Brigit, and Odin shuffling next to him. What a wonderful day he'd had! Enjoying a delicious lunch with the woman he loved, and now this. Getting to use his wealth powers happened so rarely these days.

"You are talented, but why be so theatrical about it!" Ah, Odin. Grouchy as usual, bringing him back to earth and dimming his internal glow, but nothing could ruin this lovely day. Lucky smiled and didn't comment, so Odin continued, "Glowing in public! And using magic! Unnecessary. You could have handed the girl the gift as we left."

"I can only grant wealth to the deserving through the belief of the people, so I must be theatrical for mortals to still trust I'm out there helping the community."

Brigit smiled. "I'm impressed. I didn't know you could still do that trick. How much money was in the pouch?"

He considered how to describe it as they approached the dock. "Depends on the person," he said finally. "The magic knows how worthy they are."

Odin grunted goodbye and flashed away with a tiny pop.

"Ha! And he says I show off," remarked Lucky with a smile.

Lucky's distractions melted away when he glimpsed Brigit's shining eyes. "I think you show off the perfect amount."

She was so close to him. At the same height, it seemed easy and natural when she leaned in and briefly kissed him.

Amy

"Good morning, beautiful! Breakfast is nearly ready." Robin waved Amy over to the table.

The cooking bacon smelled extraordinary. Soft music was playing and the table already contained a big bowl of scrambled eggs, a carton of orange juice, and a basket of bananas.

Instead of checking into the hotel again last night, Robin had brought her to his apartment. She hadn't protested. Not even a little. Their ship adventure was over, but maybe a new experience was beginning.

Examining the spread of food on the table, she jumped when the doorbell rang. "Is this just for the two of us? Who could that be?"

"She was upset, so I invited Piper over. Maybe you could have a talk? Girl-to-girl or something."

"Noooo. She's so baby hungry," Amy stage whispered. "She's absolutely the person I don't want to see right now."

"Too late if she's already at the door, it'll be okay." He grabbed a dish towel to dry his hands as he went to welcome her into his home, and Amy swiftly dashed to their bedroom. Finding fresh clothes and finger-combing her hair, she allowed herself one big deep sigh of frustration, then she made her way back out to the front room plastering on what she hoped was a welcoming smile.

She'd avoided her new friend after the visit with Clara. It all sounded fine when they chatted about it in theory, but Piper had reached out a couple times and Amy wasn't sure she was ready to talk about what Piper wanted. How would magic change her?

Robin excused himself and returned to the kitchen, leaving her with Brigit and Piper. "I'll get straight to the point. I still want you to become a goddess to help me have a baby."

Amy shrugged. "But I don't see how I can help."

"I want MacLir's baby. We discovered as the goddess of love, I represent the first stage of womanhood, the maiden. As such, I absolutely cannot become pregnant. Also, I can't change the goddess I am or the magic I was given, it's set. Worse, MacLir is not human and has never had a child before. One of Brigit's minor abilities is fertility, but even she can do nothing for us."

Amy shrugged again. "So? What can I do?"

Piper leaned forward eagerly. "You have the gift of strong belief. Stronger than even most humans with the gift. It helps you be successful in the human world and is truly powerful in the Otherworld. If you were to become a goddess of fertility, you would only have to believe I'd become pregnant, and I could! And you would be able to help so many other women too!"

"I understand you are excited," began Amy, trying to find the best words to make Piper understand. Finally, she wrinkled her nose and said what was on her mind. "Childbirth is messy, painful, and scary. How could you possibly ask me to put other women through this?"

"The end result. It's all worth it," said Piper, the smile spread across her face part hopeful and part smug.

Amy snorted, sounding much like Clara. "So you say, but I don't think you are hearing me. I have lots of sisters and some have almost died in pursuit of having children." The thought of it all made Amy feel like something was crushing her chest.

Piper sat back and considered this, then shook her head. "It will be fun, you'll see. I was in despair of ever having a child. Then I saw Robin with you and I knew what you could become. I've seen your baby and guided you two together because I'm sure you'll make an amazing goddess when you see how much fun a child is."

Amy's eyebrows shot up. "You pushed us together so I'd have a child?"

"Guided, not pushed. And yes, that was kind of the reason. After I met you, I realized that you might not want a baby. But you could still give me one, if you chose to become a goddess."

Robin returned in time to hear the end of the conversation. "Did you know about this?" Amy demanded of Robin, waving at Piper.

Robin denied any knowledge of Piper's plans as the goddess of love bounced halfway out of her seat. "It would be fine if Amy wanted a baby too," said Piper with a reassuring smile. "Amy would be happy about her baby. I've seen it."

No one smiled back. "I know how your power works," said Robin. "Your vision was one possible moment of happiness. You didn't see her whole life."

Piper shrugged, and doubt flickered across her face. Amy recognized the single-minded attitude from when Clara was hyperfocused on a specific outcome and tried to remember Piper was not uncaring of their feelings, only intent on her goals.

In the uncomfortable silence as they sat at the table for breakfast, Brigit finally chose to speak. "I was told you had asked about other ways to help Piper. If you don't like the title Goddess of Motherhood, what would you prefer?"

Amy gratefully grasped at this slight change in topic. "Could I pick anything?"

Brigit smiled. "Probably. But if you want to help Piper, it would need to tie into fertility. Like my healing magic does."

A jumble of emotions bounced around her mind, so Amy closed her eyes and breathed deeply. Her thoughts floated along a stream of possibilities. She pictured all the hobbies she loved. Creative writing, playing piano, and doing trick riding with her horse. None of those had anything to do with fertility. She inwardly sighed, feeling like nothing in her life was suited to motherhood, then took another deep breath and reminded herself she was trying out positivity these days. Be positive. Be brave. Clara's words. Clara who had always been brave. Jumping into marriage despite her doubts. Pouring all her creativity into raising happy imaginative children.

Creativity. That was the link. From writing to music to childrearing. People chose where to pour their creativity from day to day.

"Creativity." Amy's eyes lit with excitement at her choice.

"Creativity?"

"Goddess of Creativity. That's my choice."

"There has never been a Goddess of Creativity." Brigit pointed out.

"Then I'll be the first."

"It's very you," said Robin, around a mouthful of eggs. "I'm worried, though. It's too dangerous to take you back to the Otherworld for the ceremony."

"Why dangerous? I still don't fully understand that."

Robin hung his head and poked at his bacon. "What if you stopped believing in pixies and every tiny fae winked out of existence? What if you stopped believing in all faeries? That includes me. We don't know how powerful your thoughts are. What if you were able to kill us all?"

Even after MacLir's detailed explanation of how she could shape reality, she had not considered that it could be used as a weapon. On purpose or by accident. She wondered if she'd ever be allowed back into Robin's home.

"But how do I already have magic?" Amy asked Robin, glancing at Brigit too.

Robin placed his hand over hers, but it was Brigit who answered. "Some Tua De were given extra powers by human's believing it would happen. Powerful humans like you, gifting or enhancing the magical talents that the Tua De are born with. We mostly don't do that anymore—Piper was an exception—but mortal belief is still a strong power in the world. Even magical at times."

Amy considered that. It made sense. Humans with a strong vision were constantly reshaping the world. She believed Brigit spoke the truth. Even if she had not seen a pixie yet, Robin believed in them. So, maybe if she believed in whatever Robin told her, that would be enough? One day, she could even be allowed back into the Otherworld to become a goddess. She was actually starting to like the sound of it.

"Robin, do pixies exist?"

"Of course they do!" he said with a shrug, offering Brigit the last slice of bacon before sliding it onto his plate.

She rolled the sentence around her in her mind and tried believing in Robin's belief. "I believe in pixies," she said with conviction and was only a little amazed to discover she actually did believe it. "It worked," she told Robin.

"It did work. She really believes in them," confirmed Brigit, with a pleased smile. "Hmm… our first Goddess of Creativity. What amazingly modern times we live in."

Ian

This meeting was endless. He'd lost count of the number of ordinary people he'd had to listen to. All complaining about conditions in their home clans. Years of overpopulation had done this to them, and they'd done nothing but whine. Yet, it was still all they were doing.

If Ian was not here to fix this mess for them, what changes would they have put in place? Nothing. He wished he could return home and complete the plan without these nitwits.

"We are demanding equality for the half-mortal Tua De. We can't inherit clan caves or have skilled jobs. Instead, we're treated as little more than the captive workers we originated from. It's not our fault someone in our past was a mortal."

The views on policy he'd heard today were all over the place. These pathetic people hoped that their underground lives would be better by making him king. They were wrong. They didn't know the plan.

This man would know he was way off submitting such a claim to the new king if he did understand. Of course, only a select few knew, but the plan was to remove the humans, not live peacefully with their dirty offspring. Ian waved the man away, trying not to roll his eyes, saying, "We are making life better for our clans!"

Another man stepped forward, but Ian had mainly had stopped listening. He remembered his father coming back from meetings. Furious, his generals would dare disagree with him. He missed his father and his home. If this plan failed—his father's dream—the old man would be disappointed in him. Taking a steadying breath, he vowed again to put his whole heart into his father's plan.

Refocusing, he caught the man's last sentence. "The ban on using humans as sacrifices or as laborers has cost me household staff and hindered my use of magic. I want to make sure if I support your reign, those basic rights will be reinstated."

"Humans will finally pay for their treachery," said Ian, seemingly agreeing but internally sighing. He wished he could come out with the plan and let everyone know what was going on. Then he would not have to sit through this farce of a meeting. Publicity and marketing are what the High Court member had called them.

However, the High Court member was not among the several men sitting with him, having told Ian he was too busy today, instead leaving him in the hands of these underlings. One of them leaned toward Ian, saying, "I wonder why so few petitioners are women?"

Ian's forehead wrinkled in confusion. "I was wondering why we had any at all. After those first three, I had a word with the steward. Told him to keep them out. Why would we care what a woman has to say?"

CHAPTER 10

Amy

Amy wondered about being a goddess. What would she be in charge of? Would anyone believe in her? Human belief was key, MacLir had said. But, if she was human and knew she was not the goddess of anything, wouldn't it stop her from gaining powers? "Unless I believe in myself?" she muttered.

"What?" asked Clara, coming to crowd in next to Amy on a seat meant for one.

"Trying to wrap my mind around belief as a power is giving me a headache."

Clara shrugged. "Then don't think about it."

Easy for Clara to say. Hard for Amy to do. Thinking was the only activity she'd had all day while nervously waiting. They had picked up Clara and Brigit, then waited for the ceremonial spells and other preparations to finish. Now the time had finally arrived.

After Brigit deemed Amy still too dangerous for the Otherworld realm, Piper flew them to the earth side of a large open valley with only a few trees. Graceful hills slopped up in all directions. When the ship settled into the grass, Piper said, "Your dress is in the bathroom. You can change there."

When everyone was dressed and ready to go, they began the several minute walk toward a group of women in the distance. Piper in a deep blue dress with sparkles shining like sugar sprinkles flitting ahead. While Brigit, in beautiful shimmering silvery-white, walked next to Amy, her pure white shapeless dress flowing from her shoulders to her ankles.

"Are you sure this is the right dress?" Amy asked.

Piper giggled. "It looks exactly like mine before the faeries and magic changed it to this." She twirled gently ahead of the group in the tall high grass. Her knee-length dress swirled, and her bare feet seemed to dance on air. Her kitten floated around her in quick movements that made Amy think of a hummingbird.

Brigit, always stately, smiled at Piper and Flutter's frolicking, then strode past her to a group of people standing near a tree.

Clara gave Amy a hug, whispering, "Good luck."

"Amy, step forward," called Brigit in a low but commanding voice.

She took a steadying breath and stepped in front of six women, plus Piper on one side and Brigit on the other. She glanced behind her to see Clara sitting against the tree, watching. She examined the gathered women, young to elderly, and one heavily pregnant.

"Six strong-minded, creative women will assist us today," said Brigit, her arms raised and sleeves draping gracefully in front of her.

"Also, Brigit will play a part as she is a minor fertility deity," added Piper. "Come this way to meet our helpers." Piper led Amy toward the women, and they parted to show the plants behind them. Six seedlings were planted in a perfect circle. A seventh spot in the ring had been recently dug, but had no seedling.

Lazing on the leaves of the delicate plants were many tiny naked pixies with iridescent wings, chittering to each other with high-pitched squeaks. They rose in a buzzing cloud of bee-shaped wings when Amy appeared in front of them, so tiny and fast it was hard to see them in detail. Piper stepped into the circle of new plants and waved everyone to follow her. She positioned the human followers in a loose circle around Amy, then moved out of the way, almost to where Clara waited.

"Let it begin," said Brigit. She stepped into the circle and drew out a necklace from a hidden pocket of her gown. A y-shaped copper chain held a flat, beaten copper circle dangling at the end.

"This symbol of life was made specifically for you and the journey you make today." She clasped the lightweight necklace on Amy and announced, "Bring me the leaves."

The women must have already been briefed on the plans because they immediately stepped to the closest plant and pulled one leaf from it. Then, they deposited the leaves in Brigit's cupped hands.

Brigit shut her eyes and began to hum. Not a song Amy could describe or even remember after it stopped, but it stilled her nervous mind and made her think of hope for life. Of spring. The leaves began glowing, the dull brightness of a frosted glass globe lamp. The humming stopped, and Brigit held out the leaves.

The women each took back their leaf and placed it at the base of the plant it came from. The leaves soaked into the earth, dissolving into the freshly dug soil.

Brigit left the circle. Standing outside it, she raised her hands above her head and clapped once. The loud sound in the silent valley echoed. A signal.

The plants began to grow at a rapid speed. The pixies sprang into action, flying around and around the plants, drawing a green color from them and circling Amy to weave the green magic of thriving seeds into her dress. At first, the dress was pale green, like a new seedling, but as the plants grew, the pixies pulled a darker green from the quickly unfurling leaves until it ended in the deep green tones of a summer forest.

The six plants became six giant trees growing so close together they blocked most of the sunlight. The spot with no tree had grown low ground cover flowers. Light streamed in through the one gap in the trees, shining on dust motes, little bugs, and the cloud of pixies. Brigit was blocked from view, her part done, but the pixies continued.

They circled the six women, pulling from them a thick copper color which they carried and brought toward Amy. She held in both panic and wonder as they swarmed around her, streaks and swirls of copper appeared on her newly green dress without a speck of white left.

When the copper color was drained from their cloud, they continued to fly around her, pouring power into her being, using the copper jewelry and copper streaks on the dress as conduits. Amy was unnerved to feel those points warm on her skin as raw power flowed through the pixies into her. She sensed it coming from the soil and air, connecting her to the island under her feet.

When they were finished, the pixies flew into the treetops, quickly disappearing from view inside the canopy. Amy stood there, crackling with power but unsure what to do next.

"Goddess, step forward out of the faerie ring. Come out to greet the afternoon light," called Brigit.

Amy stepped over the carpet of flowers in the opening of the trees, careful not to crush any of the tiny upturned petals. Once on the other side, the wild power of the island dissolved into her, like the glowing leaves had in the soil. It tingled across her skin and soaked into her bones. Amy let out the breath she'd been holding, glad it was over, her body back to normal again. Almost.

The power that had thrummed through Brigit's voice before was gone as she explained, "You'll see what people want to pour their creativity into. These women are like you, they have a strong belief in themselves, and in the world as they see it. They believe that you'll become a goddess of creativity and be able to grant people the creative future they seek. By seeing what people want to pour their creativity into, you'll craft that future for them through your beliefs."

One woman stepped forward. Her trendy, short sleeveless sundress showed off the curves of a woman not much older than Amy herself. She stopped an arm's length away and said, "Goddess of Creativity, I would like to have a baby."

When the words were spoken, the power now simmering in Amy soared back to the surface. As a new magic-user, she was unprepared for the mental pictures crowding her brain. The first vision was of this woman pregnant, nearing birth. And she was very clearly happy. No, not just happy, but positively overjoyed at the life growing inside her. Transitioning to a second vision of a toddler, blowing bubbles with his loving mother, Amy believed the new fate she watched would be good for this mother and her future son. The possible tomorrows solidified around the woman, and the visions released her.

"It's done. You'll have a child," Amy told the woman, who started sobbing in relief through her smiles and stepped backward into the line of followers. Amy grinned, this new ability to create was as fun as any new trick she'd learned on her horse.

A second woman hurried forward. She had dark short hair, a kind smile, and an athletic build. Desire rolled off of her, and she didn't even need to speak to trigger the visions.

The first showed the woman struggling to get an experiment to work, then the next glimpse of a future showed this research scientist succeeding with her ambitious goals. Amy believed in this confident, clever woman.

"You will help many people with your discoveries," Amy said, giving her a heartfelt smile.

After the scientist nodded a thank you and stepped back into the line, Brigit raised her hands again. This second clap was quieter, but no less a signal than the first that the ceremony was now complete.

With the tension broken, a few of the women hugged and, with a wave, walked in the opposite direction of the ship. Then, the pixies burst from the treetops and flew off in a twinkly cloud.

Amy focused on Piper, who was rocking in place from foot to foot. "My turn," Piper said. "And I want a baby."

Amy hesitated, worried about disappointing her new friend. Opening herself to the power on purpose this time, she reached out with it to Piper. And saw… nothing.

Confused, she tried again, but only saw Piper standing alone. "I don't think the visions are working," she told Brigit, glancing over at the taller woman. With her power still open, she was hit by visions of Brigit also longing for a child. In the vision she was handing a newly born infant to a smiling man with dark blue hair. Amy believed that happiness would be good for the kind soul who loved Robin so much. She believed it would happen, and the magic released her.

"Oops," said Amy. Brigit raised an eyebrow at her, but the new goddess didn't bother to explain, muttering, "Never mind, I think it's working now."

Refocusing her magic on Piper a third time, she once again saw nothing. No baby. Only a vision of Piper, standing alone on the shore's edge watching the water.

"You can't see a baby, can you?" Piper asked. "I know, because I can't either when I look into my future."

Amy wanted to give Piper a hug but knew she would not appreciate the physical contact. At a loss for anything else to do or say, she whispered, "I'm sorry."

A frown tugged at Brigit's lips. "Piper, you need to accept this won't happen for you. Even if you were not The Maiden, MacLir is an elemental. And they don't have children."

Tears pooled in Piper's angry eyes, her voice wavering between despair and hope as she said, "I won't give up and no one can make me. It doesn't mean we can't find some other way to change the future."

Lucky

Lucky had watched the entrance to offices near the court member's house for hours and now the wait was finally worth it as he observed Ian and his guards leave for a meeting. One of MacLir's other allies had tracked them to this location, but refused to go any further. If Lucky could find out who was involved or a clue to what they were planning, then teleporting into the busy offices would be worth the risk of getting seen there.

Disappearing from the hallway he reappeared at the end of it, looked both ways, and flashed again until he was standing directly in front of Ian's office door. He flashed to the other side of the door and glanced around, braced to find guards or a secretary, but he was alone.

Ignoring the shabbiness of the space with its two chairs and a desk, he moved silently to start opening desk drawers. He was not sure what he expected to find, but could not believe his luck at unrolling a scroll with every conspirator's name signed to the document. His eyebrows rose at the notable names. Everyone in the high court was listed, even

Brigit. While inspecting her delicate scrawl for any sign of forgery, his stomach sank when it looked like her writing.

The paper crinkled under his clenched fist, but he smoothed it out, rolling it back up and returning it to the drawer. Wondering if he had time to search further, his curiosity overwhelmed him and he flashed away to demand answers from Brigit. Appearing in the hallway of her infirmary entrance, he was alarmed to see two of Ian's inner circle from the list he'd read. They were leaving the infirmary and it confirmed his worst fears. They shut the door behind them and headed down the opposite tunnel from where Lucky stood.

As soon as they were out of sight, he burst into Brigit's examination room. "Why were those men here?"

"They needed medical aid."

He wished this was not happening. He desperately wanted to accept her reply, but instead he pressed further. "They looked fine to me."

Brigit shrugged. "I'm a good healer."

"Why would they come here?"

"Everyone is allowed to come here."

"Not them. They deserve some pain. They are destroying the peace and stability MacLir and the High Court have built."

Brigit stood tall, anger flickering across her face, but took a step toward him with her palms up. "I don't see any peace or stability in these tunnels. You must be blind if you do."

Shaking his head, Lucky shifted closer to Brigit, wanting to be near her. Wanting to understand what she was saying. "How could there be peace when Ian is tearing apart the traditions of the High Court and their laws?"

"No. Ian is bringing everyone together."

"Ian has given support to the Voiceless Pure and a dozen other crackpot ideas. Bringing that lot together is a terrible idea."

"All the Tuatha Dé Danann united will always be the best option for our people. Without all this opposition to each other, we can remember who the real enemy is. We can rule again."

Lucky's blood rushed to his head, boiling rage heating his cheeks until even his ears burned. "You agree with them! Don't deny it. I've heard enough. What were those men really doing here?"

She reached out as if to cup his cheek, but touched his forehead, saying, "SLEEP."

CHAPTER 11

Ian

The second session of hearing complaints was more weary-
ing than the first and Ian would refuse the next time someone suggested this idea. When the last person had trooped
through—wasting Ian's precious time—he was finally
allowed to return to his office in peace. On the way, he saw
Robin talking to one of the secretaries in the hallway near his
home. He detoured toward the boy.

"Is there a problem?" he asked smoothly, in his gentle
politician voice.

"I was checking on my application for employment in
your campaign, sir," said Robin.

"What good news, I believe it was recently accepted and
you'll be notified soon." He added a little power in his voice,
"You must step into my office for a celebration drink before
you leave."

The boy was easily influenced and quick to agree. Ian led
them to the tiny room the court member had assigned him
as an office. He seethed at being stuck here while that man
had an opulent study to sit in.

As soon as Robin was settled, drink in hand, Ian began his questioning. Pushing his power to its highest level, the boy could not resist him.

"I know this is more than a campaign job for you. Why did you apply to the inner circle?"

"To spy on you," said Robin with a sloppy grin and raised eyebrows.

Ian wished they didn't always seem drunk when he used his power of suggestion. Wondering what else to ask the boy while still in this state, he swirled the drink in his glass and took another sip.

"Why did Brigit vouch for you?"

"She loves me like a son."

Ian's irritation softened as understanding bloomed. That would do it. He'd never had a child, but often dreamed of having a son to pass on the rule of the peaceful world he was building.

Setting aside these happy visions, he refocused on everything that still needed to happen to get to that pleasant life in his dreams. The hardest part would be to steal a human baby when the time came for one. Not just any child, but a specific infant, and the clue on finding the correct infant had been so vague.

At one point, his community still had a seer who had created many prophecies. One important phrase made it into the Master Plan developed by his father, which read, "The human daughter of the sea is key to the whole plan." He still had not found this perfect foretold child, but now Ian's mind raced.

"Robin," Ian said, the spoken word saturated with persuasive power, and Robin responded with his full attention. "You must help me locate a child. If you find the daughter of the sea, you must bring me the child. You will do this for me, right?"

"Of course, sir," replied Robin. Ian dismissed the young man, who stumbled out of the room in a daze.

This might help with the missing piece or maybe not, but it was another option to finding the key to success. Ian hated trying to untangle the ranting of the seer. He was also slightly uncomfortable with the plan.

He didn't mind killing being done, but he'd never killed anyone himself. Fought in mock battles at home? Yes. Sliced off the last king's toe to make him unfit to rule? Absolutely. Ordered people killed? Frequently. Assisted the love of his life in kidnapping girls for the crow goddess to murder? Would do it again.

Killing a child with his own hands didn't sit right in the pit of his stomach.

His brain pushed that aside and brought up his last thought. Kelli. Accidentally killed by the crow goddess in one of her fits. The love he'd found right after arriving on this island had been too swiftly taken from him by fate. They'd had so little time together. Maybe it was for the best.

When he got his hands on the child, the plan would come to completion. He would not have wanted a conflicted mind while carrying out the project his father trusted him with. So, Kelli would have died anyway. And this baby would too.

A commotion roused him from his melancholy thoughts. He rose to tell the guards off for being loud, but froze at seeing Brigit's tear-stained face. Behind her, two guards carried the sleeping body of Lucky. Excitement swamped him and he smiled, swiftly moving toward the group.

"You promised," said Brigit defensively at his approach.

"I remember," agreed Ian. He didn't even need to make the promise to Brigit because he would never hurt Lucky. Ian had wondered about this man his whole life. He had not made contact since arriving at the mounds, but watched Lucky from afar. He still hoped one day they could be friends.

Leading the guards to the court member's house seemed to ease Brigit's fear, but she was still staring at him, tense and anxious. "I'll state it again," said Ian. "Since you brought him to us asleep, just like I asked, I promise he will not be killed in our care."

Brigit nodded understanding, brushing a hand across Lucky's cheek before leaving.

Ian grinned again. For weeks he had been trying to find a way to capture Lucky without hurting him. It was so easy to manipulate Brigit's feelings for the man.

Lucky's capture was the trigger he'd been waiting for on the next step of the plan. Having Brigit see they were entering the fancy home of the High Court member was another win-win. Now, Brigit assumed the High Court member was involved in the project, giving it more legitimacy in her eyes. Meanwhile, the High Court member was in for a surprise.

He shut the front door behind Brigit, then said to the guards, "Take him to the last bedroom on the right." He watched for a moment as they carried Lucky up the mansion's stairs, acting like he didn't see the butler wringing his hands next to him.

The butler finally stepped into view and declared, "I can't authorize your men to go upstairs. You must call them back until the master of the household approves it."

"It's already done now, but we can go talk to the master," said Ian icily.

"Can I take your ha-," began the butler but stopped speaking when Ian jammed the hat tighter and glared. Instead, he said, "This way, please."

Ian strode ahead of the butler and burst into the study, taking in the two men and saying, "Good, you're both here."

"I don't appreciate being ordered around," announced the stick-thin High Court member.

"Me either," agreed Ian. "That is why I'm taking charge here."

"Taking charge of what?" asked the pudgy gray-haired general of the makeshift army.

"Everything. This house, the army, the situation underground, the Tuatha Dé Danann, the High Court, and the kingship."

The court member glared down his nose with a scornful sniff. "You can't. This house is mine, and you can't be king until the court votes you in."

"Wrong. I am taking over. You can leave right now and I won't stop you."

"I'm not leaving." The ancient High Court member swiveled on his heel to return to his desk, showing his back to Ian. A mistake.

"I thought that might be your answer." Ian took three steps and stabbed the thin man in the back. Ian pulled his knife free as the man collapsed forward. It was satisfying to get rid of this old fool as his first ever murder. Easier than he'd expected.

Ian glared at the others, the dripping knife still in his hand. "Anyone else want to tell me I'm not the king?"

The butler and general shook their heads.

"The first uprising was only thirty men led by the last king. It was a ploy. The next uprising is the real one. It starts today."

Amy

Pacing in the front room was not helping her anxiety or her exhaustion. Amy had not heard from Robin in three days and he'd never disappeared for so long before.

With each passing day Robin had been more attentive to her needs, showing his affection in little ways. He kept all her favorite snacks in the kitchen, and more importantly, he never stopped planning adventures with her. He was still unsure about leaving Ireland, but encouraged her to dream. From Amazon jungles to Australian beaches to Japanese temples, he organized every detail they discovered, added every tourist trap and hotel that looked promising.

Now, her thoughts swung widely between fear for his safety and anger at his lack of contact during these nerve racking days. Panic and hope rose in her chest at the sound of the front door opening. Had she forgotten to lock it or was that Robin with a key? She crept toward the entry hallway and peeked around the corner.

Robin shut the front door and wearily took off his coat. Without a hug or explanation of his absence, he simply said, "You look tired."

"Yes. I know I look tired. I own a mirror," snapped Amy. Robin raised his eyebrows at her, and she sighed. "Sorry. I'm a little crabby today. I didn't get much sleep because you've been gone for days."

Robin hung his head and apologized too, adding, "I attended a long protest today, in the Otherworld. I'm not used to people waiting for me on this side, so I forget about the time difference."

"Clearly." Amy tried, but could not keep all the irritation out of her voice.

"I, well, I meant to message you, but… actually, I don't remember what happened. I must be tired." He tried to grin, but it fell flat when combined with his glazed eyes.

Amy led Robin to sit on the couch next to her. "Are you okay? Did you cover the protest for MacLir or for work?"

"Yes, for work," said Robin with relief. "That must be it."

He didn't sound sure of himself, but she listened as he told her about the various views of people he'd met. They fell into two groups, either supporters of MacLir or people who were sure he was the actual problem. "Most people seem to have forgotten how MacLir offered my people a home underground. After that, all the laws binding the Tua De have been created by the High Court."

The more he talked, the more Robin came back to himself, so Amy asked, "What are they upset about?"

"They want to live in the human world. Not just live there, but reconquer it and rule. Human stealing and sacrifice are against court law, and they want those rules gone as well. The other side of the argument has always been equality in jobs and living conditions. Still, because the High Court refuses to change any laws, those people are getting frustrated too and calling for the High Court to dissolve. Ian promises to give both groups what they want, so nearly every unhappy Tua De has banded together for the first time ever. They are all following Ian as a fresh new type of king. Hope for their future."

"You almost sound as if you like him too." Amy had not met Ian and barely knew the politics, but conditions must change for Robin's people from what she'd seen. Luckily he could live above ground, but what about the others? She remembered the cave with the twin boys and with a shudder compared it to the comfort she lived in with the boy she loved.

Although, was she in love? Most days she wasn't even sure what love was. Being comfortable enough to sit close and rub his back because he was stressed. Was that love? It wasn't the one-sided infatuation of her creepy cousin. It wasn't the electric sensations she'd experienced in haylofts with farm boys either. She cared about Robin and would miss him if he was not around. Was that love? Missing someone if they weren't in the same room as you?

Perhaps it was the closeness and connection they already shared? Being with Robin was comfortable. It made her happy. She could picture a future here, living in this city and traveling together. She'd decided to stay, at least for a while, and then see what the winds of fate offered her next.

CHAPTER 12

Piper

Piper placed a fresh diaper under the toddler. Carefully doing all the steps the director had shown her to make sure the baby was clean and dry. Healthy and safe. Replacing the little boy's tiny pants and hugging him close, Piper held back tears that still closed her throat up.

The ceremony failed. Well, not failed. Clearly Amy had more magic, but it was not a win for Piper. MacLir was an elemental and even if they got around her own magic restrictions, a baby was not going to happen.

Winding her way down from the nursery back to the dining hall she wondered if perhaps she should give in and adopt the next abandoned half human infant from the mounds. She'd happily take the little guy she was holding, but the director was attached and had already adopted him as her own. The other kids loved it here and she didn't want to tear them away from their friends.

The dream of having her own child was getting thin and would soon pop like a delicate soap bubble. Adopting was a good choice too, though. MacLir was happy with his foster children over the years, and she should be too… but she could not get the idea of raising MacLir's baby out of her head.

MacLir was playing don't-let-the-balloon-touch-the-floor with a group of boys almost his height, while the others sat at the table folding leftover paper or using the new supplies she brought to make bendy spiders with wiggly eyes.

The director, taking away an empty tea tray, paused and cried out, "Oh my! So many spiders are infesting this tray. Oh, no! Where did they all come from?"

The younger children gleefully giggled at their trick and the director met Piper's eyes, a shared smile in them.

"Watch out," came a call from their right. The balloon came out of nowhere and bopped the director in the face, then dropped away revealing her annoyed eyebrows. It bounced over the tea tray before slowly floating down.

"No! It's going to touch the ground!" MacLir did a dive for it, swinging his arm up to bat the balloon back into the air and falling on his rump. However, he smacked the balloon and the tea tray, which caused both to go flying. The balloon was hit by another player and returned to the game. The tea tray was not so lucky. It crashed down next to MacLir, sending plastic cups and wiggly-eyed spiders in all directions. MacLir sheepishly held up the empty glass teapot he'd caught and offered it to the director. She took it, but rolled her eyes and shook her head.

"MacLir! I made more boats! Let's have a race!" Jimmy grinned from ear to ear holding his handful of boats in imita-tion of MacLir on their last visit. "I'll race you to the bridge!"

"Hold up stort stuff." MacLir had caught sight of Piper's sad eyes and stood to give her a gentle hug. "Wanna go for a walk? You can come watch us race boats at the bridge."

Piper didn't trust herself to speak without crying, some-thing she'd done a lot these days. Nodding, she took his hand, repositioned the toddler on her hip, and followed MacLir and some of the children out to the river.

A breeze blew up from the ocean nearby, chilly yet refreshing. It cleared her mind and reminded her of everything she was grateful for. MacLir's kindness, the children, the beautiful place she lived, and the wonderfully comfortable life she enjoyed. MacLir squeezed her hand and ran off to play with the children. She laughed at his eagerness to join the boat race. When the boats were dropped over the railing, and everyone raced to the other edge, Piper cheered MacLir's boat on and groaned with him when he lost.

On the next start, Jimmy's boat got stuck on a rock and MacLir grinned at him, using his power to swirl salt in the water under the boat so it flowed away and quickly rejoined the others. Piper was surprised there was enough salt in this river for MacLir to control it, but then she remembered how the saltwater reached up to meet the river flowing down to it. The mix of salty and fresh water created the estuary under the bridge.

An idea flitted through her mind. Only half a thought, but she clung to it. MacLir represented an element in human form and she was human. Elemental and human, different but the same, like the salt and fresh water in the estuary. What if it was possible for the two to mix like it did here? Some creative way to merge the two elements together.

The answer hit her so hard she staggered back into the railing. MacLir's concerned face came into view, but she ignored what he said as he held her and the baby upright. She had it. The path forward she'd been looking for suddenly became possible with Amy's ceremony. For this new idea, a goddess of creativity was even better than a goddess of fertility. She remembered MacLir telling her his origin story, how he walked out of the waves on his island. Created by the belief of the people in an ocean god.

It was all about belief. It always had been.

"MacLir! I have an idea. I need to talk to Amy."

Amy

"So, you want me to merge your elements and create you an instant baby?" Amy thought she understood the request and she was not sure how it would be done. Although, she was eager to try.

"We'd have to do it in the Otherworld, but we'd do it on MacLir's island. MacLir was born on his island, so if this will work anywhere, it's there," Piper rambled on.

MacLir smiled encouragingly at the two of them, and Robin was thoughtfully quiet as the girls planned out the ceremony.

"It's easy for MacLir, we'll simply use saltwater, but what can we use for you?" Amy considered earthy human things, like soil.

"Hair."

"What?"

"My hair. Did you know your whole DNA is in your hair?"

"I… yeah, I guess that could work." Amy agreed that would be an ideal way to get specifically Piper's side instead of anything from the human realm. Yet, how would she merge water and hair?

"Yes! It must work," Piper bounced in place. "Can we try now? Like, right now?"

Robin had a whole evening planned for them, with dinner reservations. She even had a new dress to wear. The hope and pleading in Piper's eyes dissolved her hesitation. She could go on a date anytime, but she paused to glance at Robin who gave a slight nod of agreement with a soft smile.

"Sure. Let's go," said Amy, and Piper squealed in delight.

Gathering a few items and an overnight bag was quick, and soon they headed out the door. Only a few steps away from the apartment, the street melted away like runny watercolors, and Amy now stood in a broad grassy area next to Wave Sweeper.

Scanning the incredible view of the expansive empty land she was overwhelmed with the beauty of it. "Where are we?"

"The Otherworld, the Sidhe Realm. The world of elementals, like me. And others."

The air was clear. She had never thought about air before, but the air in this place was transparent. She climbed the ladder and could see even further in the distance. From the ship's height as she looked over the railing, she could see individual blades in the waving emerald green grass spreading for miles to meet a deep blue sky.

"Where is everyone? Why don't people live here instead of in the caves and tunnels?"

"Two reasons," replied MacLir while giving Piper a hand to help her over the ship's edge. "The Sidhe Realm is everywhere. It is the realm of the elementals and a haven for magical beings, shielded from often dangerous mortals. But the barrier is thin, too thin to support mass on both sides in the same place. Nature can live here, but if you try to build a house in the same spot as a building in your realm, you would have problems."

"What's the second reason?"

MacLir pointed far in the distance, "Do you see the dark smudge on the horizon? Those are trolls guarding their territory. They also hunt deer for their dinner. If they find an elf, human, or other creature, they'll eat it for dessert."

"But I saw trolls in the faerie mounds," Amy pointed out.

"Vegetarians."

The flight to the island was quick, and soon a tiny outcropping of rock came into view. A few trees stood tall behind a hut, next to a patch of sand, protected from the harsh waves by rocky tide pools. A pig pen was constructed next to the hut, the mud inside it hardened and crusted over from disuse.

"Are you having any luck finding your pig?" Amy hesitated, but was too curious about the situation and asked, "Has anyone… died yet?"

A rare frown showed MacLir's worry. "No one has died, but we're getting close to running out of our stock of jerky, and I've got no leads on where they are keeping Pig. We must keep hoping for the best outcome."

They were distracted when Piper brought out a hooded baby basket with handles. A blanket spread along the bottom cushion was bunched at the sides, waiting to fold a baby into it. The sight made Amy nervous. What if she was not able to create a baby from merged elements? Piper seemed so sure it would work, bouncing around the deck. Amy could not understand Piper's endlessly jolly outlook about her baby. Or any child. Although her happy attitude was annoying, Amy smiled at her hope. If Piper could still have this much hope, so could Amy.

The ship was left by the tide pools and everyone made their way to the soft sand beach. Robin moved out of the way to watch, sitting with his back against the hut. Amy missed his comforting presence, and wished he'd stayed nearby.

Piper put the basket in the sand and stared at Amy expectantly. Now what? She tried to remember the plan. "Oh, we need your hair." She glanced around as if expecting to see something sharp, and in fact did. Scissors lay in Robin's outstretched hands. She smiled her thanks at his forethought, and Piper hurried over to grab them.

"How much do you need?" she asked Amy, who shrugged in answer. Piper cut off several locks and leaned forward to put them in the basket, but MacLir's hand stopped her.

"Hold on. Look." A selkie galumphed up the beach toward them, dragging a piece of seaweed. "I asked him to get it." MacLir bowed in thanks to the selkie who nodded and disappeared back in the waves.

Taking Piper's hair, MacLir wrapped it into the seaweed, creating a bundle he placed in the basket, and folded the blanket edges over it. Then he lifted a bubble of saltwater from out of the ocean, bringing it to hover in front of them. The water bubble burst over the basket, soaking the blankets and the packet of seaweed beneath.

Amy began to think. Hard.

She considered Piper's joy of children and her single-mindedness, then thought of MacLir's playfulness. How the ocean is mischievous, when a gust of wind blows off a hat, or spray of sea foam makes a deck slippery. She remembered her sister's new infants. How their hair was a gentle fuzz and their tiny toes no larger than peas. She believed all of these ideas would merge with Piper's DNA and MacLir's link to the sea. She believed a baby made from both of them would replace the seaweed packet in the basket.

Wind twirled around the island and the sound of roaring tides grew louder. A spear of sunlight shone through the clouds onto the basket and the blankets began to shift and swell. When the winds died down and the clouds reformed, Amy clapped firmly once like she'd seen Brigit do and the crackly feeling in the air faded away.

She glanced at Piper who was looking at MacLir, but now looked at Amy and they both looked at MacLir. Robin came to stand next to Amy, taking her hand and squeezing it. No one moved toward the basket where the blanket wiggled. Finally, Piper knelt in the sand and unwrapped the edge to reveal a tiny perfect infant, with a pale face and blonde hair fuzz.

"A daughter of the sea," whispered Robin.

CHAPTER 13

Piper

It worked. The baby was real and laying in front of her, its waving hand caught a passing toe and grabbed on. The infant's unfocused blue eyes blinked and glanced around. Piper tenderly wrapped the baby back in the blanket and picked her up, standing to move closer to MacLir. They touched foreheads as they stared down at the tiny wonder.

Piper handed her to an equally speechless MacLir. He kissed the top of the baby's head. "Hello, little one." For a moment her eyes focused on him, then shifted away.

He held the baby out and Robin accepted the bundle from MacLir. "She's so beautiful!"

"Yep, it's a baby," said Amy, raising her hand to stop Robin from passing the infant to her.

Robin chuckled and gave the baby back to Piper asking, "Do you know what you want to call her?"

Names? She glanced at MacLir. "It's totally up to you," he said.

Piper had lists of possible names that she'd gathered. She cycled through them trying to find one that fit. "What about… Emily?"

Everyone let out a gentle noise of agreement, and even Amy softened enough to say, "It's perfect." Piper was pleased they liked her name and it did fit. She placed Emily back in the basket and handed it to MacLir to get on the ship.

Piper's heart stopped when MacLir called forth a wave and handed the basket to the water. It surged upward and placed the basket on the deck a moment before depositing MacLir next to it. Everyone else followed, preferring the conventional way up the ladder.

"Where now?" MacLir asked Piper with a grin.

"Brigit! We must show her the baby. Now I feel bad we didn't invite her along."

MacLir shrugged. "She won't mind. She'll know you didn't exclude her on purpose."

On the way to the mounds they stopped to show two groups of selkies and told them they were headed to show Brigit. In the great kitchens there was another delay while Ginger, the head cook, fawned over Emily and provided them with some milk to feed her. Piper appreciated the gesture—she had not even thought of food yet—and wished they'd brought the basket with them to store the offerings.

By the time they made it to Brigit's infirmary a large crowd had gathered to see and greet the new legend. "Selkies," snorted MacLir. "Such gossips."

Brigit was at the head of the crowd, and stretched out her arms as soon as they were in sight.

"This is Emily." MacLir passed the bundle to Brigit, who shifted her into an experienced hold.

Brigit's eyes shone with wonder. "You did it. I don't know how, but this is the first child of an elemental that I've ever heard of." She softly stroked the baby's cheek with one finger, repeating, "You did it."

"It was Amy," said Piper proudly, "our new Goddess of Creativity!"

"Well, it was your idea," Amy pointed out.

"A group effort," said MacLir. "Three cheers for my daughter, Emily!"

The whole crowd cheered as requested, and music started in one corner of the well-lit rectangular cavern. The gauzy curtains and sick beds were pushed to the edges of the room as the party broke out. Piper became drawn into a conversation with a selkie who helped out at the orphanage, but didn't miss that the room was quickly filling with even more people.

Piper caught one glimpse of Robin leaning against the door by the wall, a deep frown on his flushed face and a tear in his sad eyes. She moved toward him to ask if he was feeling unwell, but the gap in the crowd closed and by the time she made it through, he was gone.

Ian

Ian tensed at seeing a figure come toward him out of the shadows, until he recognized the man as Robin. Ian had not seen Robin since right before the uprising that made him king. It had been partially effective, but many of MacLir's allies remained uncaptured, including the sea god himself. Ian would have to sort that out, but it wouldn't matter until the baby was found.

Ian waited in the silence, while Robin stood in front of him sweating and shaking, seeming incapable of speech, but unwrapped the blankets in his arms. A baby. Ian's heartbeat picked up. Was it the baby foretold? He'd almost forgotten tasking Robin with bringing him a baby, but was it the right one?

"Whose baby is this?"

Robin clutched the buddle in his arms closer to his chest, his semi-glazed eyes glaring, and pressed his lips together.

"Speak man, what have you brought me?"

Robin's jaw clenched, but he couldn't resist the force in Ian's words. "This is MacLir's daughter, born this morning. A human daughter of the sea."

Ian's mind whirled with relief and delight. The prophecy must mean this infant. A human and elemental child? Unheard of. Perfect for the sacrificing ceremony. "Follow me," Ian demanded.

Shaking harder with the effort of resisting Ian's influence, Robin took one step then stopped. A tear rolled down his cheek.

Ian pulled even more power to him and fused it into his words. "Robin. Follow me. Bring the child."

Robin should not have been able to withstand, but still hesitated for a moment before his mind gave way, and he meekly plodded behind Ian.

His father had been so sure the child would be found in the tunnels that Ian had not ordered any human infants stolen. He'd waited. Prepared and planned, yet sat on his hands. Now, with every step forward, Ian was more sure than ever this was the right child. Not only found at the perfect moment but also the daughter of the sea, powerfully magical but without any Tuatha Dé Danann heritage.

Although his preference was to take the child right to the ceremony, everything needed more time to get rolling. The uprising had been successful, that had been an important step. Anyone who disagreed with him was either killed, captured, or escaped, but he still needed a few more people out of the way.

Luck had blessed him twice today, as a rumor that all of MacLir's allies were gathering in Brigit's infirmary. If it was preparation for an attack, they would be surprised. He'd already sent a team to seize anyone in Brigit's space, in case the rumor was true. After that, he only had a few more pieces to get into place.

His boots squelched in the mud of this tunnel. It was undignified. He'd order it fixed when he had a chance. There should be no mud around the front door of his home. He was the king. Or, maybe he would not bother with repairs here. Soon he would not need to worry about the tunnels. Finally, after centuries of mud and darkness, he'd lead his people into the sunlight.

Killing the High Court member had been a good start, but now with the child ready, he could give the signal and all the plans would launch. It should only take a few days, and he could be in an above-ground castle by the end of the week. King of everyone and everything.

Although, Ian was still a little unsure of how it would work. He would lead this group of his people into the light. That was the clearest part of the plan. Then his foster brother, Tamlin, already also a High King, would lead the group from his home, bringing them here to Ireland. Although, would they both be High King? When he'd tried to ask for clarification on this point, he was ignored by his father's generals.

They arrived at the home of the dead High Court member. Now it was his home, Ian reminded himself. He waved over two goons, annoyed at being pulled from their flirting with the secretaries, but they still obeyed. Ian smiled. Everyone always obeyed. Now, with the child finally found, everyone would continue to follow him forever.

He glanced at Robin's glazed eyes, wondering how to keep him silent on where the baby had been taken. He could simply kill him. However, Brigit loved this boy, so it would be best to hide Robin somewhere out of the way for now, in case they needed her help again.

"Hand me the child." Through the tunnels, his control over Robin must have slipped. The man was standing still, but panicked, scared, and angry. He was shaking from resisting with every ounce of willpower. He didn't hand over the baby, so Ian sighed, pulled in more power, and said, "ROBIN."

The man went still. Ian plucked the bundle of blankets from his arms, then nodded to his guards. One knocked Robin over the head and they dragged his unconscious body up the stairs.

Amy

The celebration became more crowded every minute. MacLir's friends in the mounds had been contacted and they were stopping by to congratulate him. Ginger was bustling around bringing food from the kitchens and grinning proudly. She held out a tray of fruit tarts to Amy, who hesitated before accepting one. She'd been warned about fae food linking her to the Otherworld.

"Is that human food? It smells good."

"Oh yes, I've been careful only to bring human food in here." Ginger winked. Which didn't reassure Amy. She accepted a tart, but was careful not to eat it. Not sure what the wink meant, she was not taking any chances at getting stuck in the Otherworld.

Piper twirled over and joined them, grabbing a tart and tossing it whole into her mouth. "Have you seen Brigit?"

"Yes," said Ginger, "I've spent the last half-hour chatting with her while cooking the human food. She's in the kitchen."

"Does she have Emily?"

"Of course not, the baby is with MacLir."

Amy shook her head. "I just saw MacLir, but he doesn't have her."

"Robin?" asked Piper, starting to look alarmed.

"Nope," said Ginger. "I saw him leave ten minutes ago, heading down the west tunnel. I figured he was gathering more people."

Warm and prickly sensations shivered down Amy's spine, and a sense of doom washed over her. Something didn't fit. Finally, the pieces fell into place. "If Piper is here, Robin is gone, Brigit in the kitchen, and MacLir is over there… who has the baby?"

A scream sounded in the tunnel and before Amy could process it, men stormed into the infirmary. She felt someone grab her hand and looked up to see MacLir's grim face as he tugged them straight through a dirt wall into the outside corridor.

"There he is! Get them," someone yelled from behind her, but MacLir was already running and dragging her along. She caught a glimpse of Piper on his other side, then focused her attention on her feet and not tripping to keep up with MacLir's speed.

Footsteps pounded behind them. They had a good head start, but would it be enough? Amy pictured the tunnel wall behind them, imagining that it had thick stone doors that came out of the wall and met in the middle, trapping their pursuers. She heard a grinding noise as the stone obeyed her, slowly closing off the tunnel.

MacLir glanced back at the noise and paused, grinning at the shocked faces of the attacking Tua De as they skidded to a halt. Then the doors finished shutting and all was quiet.

"You'll have to come back and fix this tunnel you know," mused MacLir, running his hands over the carved stone door.

Amy didn't want to come back to this tunnel, or maybe even any of the faerie mounds. She wondered how she could fix it now, without letting that mob catch them. A grinding sound and pop to their right caused Piper and MacLir to laugh. A lever had appeared next to the new doors. Amy grinned smugly. "You can open the doors later, MacLir, when it's safe."

MacLir immediately sobered from his laugh. "It might not be safe to return for a long time." He turned to Piper, opening his mouth to say more, but then snapped it shut, his eyes going wide as he looked to her and then to Amy and then around at the floor.

"I don't have Emily," Piper whispered. "She's missing."

CHAPTER 14

Piper

"I can't go searching around the mounds right now. It would only rile people up more." MacLir leaned back against the ship bench and put an arm around Piper. She shrugged it off and kicked his shin. "I didn't say we wouldn't look," he added. "Only that I can't go."

Piper rolled her eyes toward him, but knew he was right. A lot of whispering had caught her attention at the unplanned party when they went to show the baby to Brigit, and she'd received a surprising amount of hostile stares on the way to the infirmary. MacLir had been attacked not long ago, and it was probably only Brigit's presence that kept the same from happening to Piper.

Staring off into the distance and rocking slightly, her arms felt so empty. Emily was real and had been cuddled next to her only that morning. Now, neither of them could search the tunnels, and Amy, as a human, would not be any safer right now. Where did that leave them? "Has Lucky called back yet?"

MacLir sighed. "No. Actually, I have not heard from him in a few weeks. I figured he was busy, but now I'm getting worried. What if he was captured?"

"Do you think that's what happened to Robin? Captured?" Amy asked, making Piper jump at the sound. In her misery, she'd forgotten her friend was there with them.

"Robin must be captured," MacLir agreed. "He would not have wandered off without returning to us, and the attack was soon after that."

In focusing on the conversation for a moment, Piper wondered why MacLir's tone had softened, and noticed Amy was upset. It made sense that Amy would be worried for Robin, since he was probably hurt or captured. Unless… Piper remembered Robin's sad expression at the party and how the attack happened soon after he disappeared, and sucked in a breath. "Are you sure Robin didn't start the attack or take Emily? He was your agent, right? Your spy? What if he was, I don't know, a double agent?"

Amy shook her head, but her shoulders drooped. "He couldn't be. Even if he was, he wouldn't steal a baby, right?"

Piper wanted to fall apart, but there was no time. She temporarily pushed away the dizziness she felt and asked, "What do we know for sure?"

"All the faerie mounds are in chaos," offered MacLir.

"Emily is missing," whispered Amy.

"Lucky and Robin are presumed missing as well," added MacLir.

Usually, lists helped Piper, but this one was simply depressing, crushing her under its weight of hopelessness. Exasperated, she asked, "Why would anyone steal an infant?"

MacLir shrugged and put his arm around her again. "Whoever did this has an unknown motive, but more importantly, the access to information to pull off a kidnapping directly from Brigit's infirmary."

They paused to think about that enormous breach of trust until Piper's phone rang, making them all jump. She glanced sideways at the usually unflappable MacLir, who grinned sheepishly. If he was on edge enough to startle at a phone call, the situation must be dire. She tried to push all the worry into the deepest corner of her mind and handed the phone to MacLir, saying, "It's Brigit."

While MacLir listened, Piper's mind wandered and anxiety threatened to overwhelm her. "Flutter," Piper called to the kitten's mind, trying to get her attention. "Come help me for a moment."

The cat sauntered out of the hallway, where she'd been dozing, and went directly to Piper. "You are so sad." The kitten's words were a somber whisper in her mind. Jumping into her lap, Flutter nudged Piper's hand, demanding a chin scratch before rolling on her back for belly rubs. Although tears dripped from her cheeks onto her shirt, Piper felt calmer as she rhythmically petted the cat.

Piper could not grasp how she could be calm at all. She felt… detached. Maybe it was shock or perhaps she just wasn't like most other people. Piper would never understand humans. She seemed to fit in better with the Tua De than she ever had with her own kind.

Her own kind? Where had that come from? She must have spent too much time in the mounds to start picking up their phrases. Their leader, Ian, was offering all kinds of promises she didn't know how he would deliver. Something about that line of thinking tried to get her attention, but the connection slipped away before she could pin down why it might be important.

Turning her mind back to the phone conversation, she strained to listen to Brigit, but only heard MacLir when he finally replied, "Actually, Lucky's not answering his phone. Maybe I should make an announcement in the great hall? Asking if anyone knows anything about this?"

He paused to listen, then said, "I still have loyal friends in the mounds, like you."

Piper hoped it was true. The faerie head cook had told her a rumor that all the outlying groups had merged into one opposition group with Ian as their king. They wanted to rule the humans. If all the Tua De thought similarly, humans would be plunged into war. Or, if the Tua De were still split about fifty-fifty on this issue, there would be civil war in the mounds. Either way, this would end in disaster for a lot of people.

Urgent but unintelligible words came through, and MacLir replied, "All of them were captured from the infirmary? Everyone?" Another pause. "Fine, you are right. An announcement would be dangerous."

Piper was relieved MacLir was listening to Brigit. She always had such wise counsel. She could understand how Lucky could fall head over heels for the healer. She'd seen some confusing bits of their romance, but decided it didn't need her help to progress.

"Oh, a lead? Yes, I've heard the northeast clan are acting strange. Yes, that is odd," agreed MacLir. "We'll go check it out right now."

Amy

When MacLir parked Wave Sweeper on the beach, Amy recognized the normal air of the human realm. "How do people not see the ship?"

"People believe what they want to believe. Friends of fae will see it for what it is, others might see something else," MacLir said with a shrug, pulling Piper to her feet and leading her to the rope ladder.

The rocky beach they stood on was familiar. The cliffs, the driftwood, and the pounding waves. Then she remembered. This was the cave she'd visited with Robin. She ignored the drop in her stomach at the thought of him missing, and maybe never seeing him again. "This can't be the place, it's not right," she told MacLir.

The waves closest to MacLir flowed higher on the beach than the others, splashing playfully around his ankles. Glancing around the same way she did, as if he expected to see a clue, he said, "It looks fine to me."

"The beach is okay. I mean, the last time we were here, the cave was empty except for a couple of boys and their mom, and even they're probably long gone. The whole community moved out."

"Maybe they returned?" Piper asked hopefully. She took MacLir's hand, and they picked their way along the beach, leaving Amy to follow.

She scowled at their backs. They were trying to help, but it was the coward's way out. Their baby had been stolen in the main mounds. Robin had been captured there too. Because they were both too scared to go where people were, they'd dragged her here, to explore an empty cave on the word of a healer who probably didn't know anything about it.

She stomped behind them, kicking everything in sight. Each strike of her foot sent shells and rocks flying. They slammed into each other with satisfying thuds and clacks. Then, when she kicked a firm piece of driftwood and only hurt her toes, she continued fuming, but stopped taking it out on the beach.

She'd been shocked to hear Robin was missing. Now? The shock had evaporated and she was angry. No, enraged. Everything was ruined. Her future with Robin was out of reach, and how dare anyone mess with Piper and MacLir on such a joyous day?

True she could make another baby, but even she knew another child wouldn't replace one who'd been lost. She was furious there was no clear path forward to fix this. And no one knew where to find Robin or Emily. Except here, apparently. A dead-end, she was certain of it. Amy trailed after Piper, who had let go of MacLir's hand and now followed him into the narrow tunnel entrance, where her certainty faltered.

The many thread-bare curtains she remembered from her last visit still blocked the full view of the cave, but this time anticipation hung in the cave's air and gave her goosebumps. Even though she could not see anyone, Amy was sure this was not an empty cave. Now she wished they had brought more people to check out this possible lead. MacLir was overconfident to think they could explore this cave alone. Even if it was barely more than an outpost, the faerie mounds were all rioting today. Despite being so far from the others, this was still a faerie mound.

From the tense lines of the shoulders in front of her, it seemed MacLir and Piper also sensed the hostility in the unnatural quiet. They moved together, hand in hand, deeper into the muddy disorder. Amy wanted to stop them. To leave. Yet, if this was their only lead, what if they came back with more people and it was too late?

In her pause to think, she'd lost sight of the couple and rushed to follow, peeking behind the curtains near her. She didn't see them, so she checked another and another with no luck. Almost calling out for them, she hesitated. Something waited. She could still sense the ominous energy in the air.

Instead of shouting for her friends, she climbed a table to peek above the curtains. She was in time to see an uncountable number of men and women rushing toward the cave's center, where MacLir and Piper were still weaving through the maze of fabric. A trap. It could be nothing else. Soldiers in ragged uniforms, waiting for their quarry.

She reminded herself she had powers here in the Otherworld. After all of Robin's warnings and Brigit's careful training to rein in her thoughts, she was still terrified to use her belief magic, but like the tunnel earlier, these were desperate times. Casting around for ideas, she decided to show MacLir what was coming.

She examined the ropes holding the curtains, seeing all the places they were pulled too tight. Imagining hundreds of years of weather damage on these ropes would cause them to buckle under the strain, she believed seawind and salty air had eroded their strength.

So, that's what happened.

The ropes darkened with age. Next, unbearably loud cracks split the air as they snapped apart. Frayed ends dropped to the ground and took their cargo of curtains with them.

Suddenly the cave was huge, now that it was wide-open. With a roar, the army charged toward the pair exposed far in front of Amy, in the middle of the cavern.

MacLir pushed Piper toward Amy, shouting, "Go back! Run! I'll be right behind you!"

Amy reached the entrance first, but could see Piper would not make it. MacLir was fighting off the first wave, but a man ahead of the others had made it through and aimed straight for Piper. Amy ran toward him with an angry shout. "Get away from her!"

Piper continued to run past Amy and years of practicing self-defense with her dad kicked in. As the man leaned forward to try to tackle her, Amy grabbed his shoulders and brought her knee up. At the crunch of his nose breaking, he backed away a few steps.

Not taking her eyes off him, she settled into a braced stance. When he charged her again, she crouched a little lower and stepped to one side, bringing her palm up. All the force of her arm connected with his chin. His momentum, still trying to move him forward, was thrown off balance, and he landed flat on his back in the mud.

Amy took this chance to follow Piper. At the entrance, she paused to follow Piper's horrified gaze and saw MacLir being overwhelmed by sheer numbers. He caught Piper's eye and shouted, "Run!" Then he fell out of sight under the crush of bodies.

Pulling Piper from the scene, Amy dragged her back into daylight and toward the ship. Stumbling through the fist-sized rocks on the beach was slow, and only halfway along, the first soldiers appeared behind them.

"We aren't going fast enough," said Amy. Ignoring Piper's tears, she pushed the other girl ahead of her, but knew they would not make it to the ship before the enemy advanced behind them.

"Look," said Piper. The calm waves shifted, swelled, and rose a few feet higher up the beach. When the waves receded, the beach was full of seals. Faster than Amy's eye could track it, they transformed into naked men and women who ran toward Piper as fast as they could get their legs under them.

The seals had seemed helpful so far, but which side were they on in today's battle? "Friend or foe?" asked Amy urgently as the seals rushed closer.

"Friend," said Piper, choking on the word through her tears. "Always friends."

The first seals to reach them ran past to hold off the army. One stopped to say, "Fia was right—you do need us. Where's MacLir?"

"In the mound, already captured," said Amy, "We're trying to get to the ship before they catch us, too."

The selkie nodded and ran to join the others in protecting their getaway. The powerful seals easily beat back the unnerved Tua De, pushing them to return to the Otherworld, but not following them into the cave. Amy watched only a moment, then moved Piper toward the ship again.

CHAPTER 15

Piper

During times of strong emotion, Piper could not concentrate enough to get the ship high in the air. Like now. Sitting cross-legged on the bench, she clenched the keys painfully tight and managed to drag the boat off the beach into the waves.

"What is happening?" Amy asked as the flat bottomed boat slowly scraped along rocks and bumped into logs.

"Shhhh," Piper replied. She barely had enough concentration to gain this foot in the air, she couldn't possibly talk as well. The image of MacLir under all the soldiers replayed in her mind and the sense of loss churned her stomach. The boat dropped, jolting her back to her task. She raised it a few inches off the ground and kept it going.

If MacLir managed to escape, she wanted to get herself to safety so he didn't have to focus on protecting them both again. She would not admit he was not coming out of the cave. Her mind showed her again, repeating images of the moment he vanished under a dogpile of uniforms. The ship crashed down again, shuddering from the impact.

This time it was in the water, so it rose on its own and drifted on the waves. Fia popped their head over the ship's edge, asking, "Need help?"

"Yes!" Amy replied for both of them.

The sea dragon's head bobbed, and the ship began to move out of the waves, drifting out to sea.

Flutter approached Piper carefully, sniffing her hand and sending, "You are hurt?" Too upset to cry or speak, or even to send a reply, Piper didn't answer. Instead, she grabbed the cat and hugged her close.

"Can't breathe," sent the cat. Piper immediately loosened the hug, and some shock wore off in the physical release of letting the cat go. She stared at the Wave Sweeper key, the two smooth gemstones sparkling inside their circular wooden casing, and began twirling the worry-stone-shaped key in her fingers. With her need to escape gone and her hands busy, she could finally think about what had happened. Evaluating it from start to finish, the pieces of the situation didn't add up.

"Amy? Did it seem like they were waiting for us?"

"Yes, I thought so."

"Why didn't you use your powers to stop them?"

"I tried to help. I believed all the ropes would fall, so you could see the enemy."

"That meant they could see us. I don't think it helped. Why didn't you kill them all?"

Amy's worried eyes went wide, then narrowed as she said, "At least I tried something. What did you do to help?" Amy was right. Piper knew it. She'd done nothing and had needed help with every part of their escape, even moving the ship away from the beach. Fia had done that.

"Fia? Are you still there?" Piper called.

"Here, my friend." The dragon's iridescent scales caught the light, flashing reflections in all directions like a disco ball.

Their chameleon-like eyes focused on the humans aboard the ship.

Piper transferred her gaze from staring at the key to Fia, asking, "Why didn't you help us?"

"I brought the selkies."

She had forgotten Fia brought the selkies, but anger flowed through Piper, prickling along her neck and down to her fingertips. "The selkies? They didn't arrive in time to save MacLir. They didn't even try!" She knew it was unfair to direct her annoyance at Fia, but could not stop herself from standing, hands on hips, and stalking toward the dragon. "How did you know we even needed help?"

"I hear things. Around." Fia huffed out a little breath, hot and fishy today, then retreated, as if backing away from Piper's fury.

"From who?" Piper demanded.

Fia's eyes tilted wildly in all directions before the dragon sank below the surface, leaving nothing but a spreading ripple on the calm ocean water, and a confused Piper staring at the sea.

Amy

"Peace with humans is impossible," shouted an old woman.

Head and eyes down, Amy followed Brigit as quickly as she could without drawing attention to themselves.

"Our golden era is back!" a man shouted, followed by a loud chorus of "Yeah!"

Her magic bottled up tight, both creativity and belief, Amy rushed on through the passageway left open for foot traffic near the active protest. Brigit was trying to get them to her infirmity, but Amy wondered if they should have simply stayed in the kitchens with the head cook, Ginger.

"Maybe we should go back?"

"Stay close," said Brigit, "you will be fine."

Amy sighed inwardly. Her new magic had done nothing to assist in finding anyone. She could make other women fertile or boost their creativity, but could not help in the search for Robin or MacLir's other supporters, who continued to go missing every day. Brigit had said that she and Ginger were the only two of MacLir's supporters not impacted. Apparently, even these wildly upset people would not hurt their best cook and only healer.

Brigit had been their rock through the days of searching, but even she was beginning to crack, becoming quieter and more reserved. Brainstorming with her on what to do next had led to this idea to try Amy's belief magic in the Otherworld.

Brigit glanced over, saying abruptly, "Robin is a good man. Were you happy living with him?"

"Of course. He's kind and cheerful…" Amy's throat tried to close up, but she continued, "he's good to me."

"I think so too." Brigit's eyes shadowed in a blank stare as if gazing inward to long ago memories. "I had a son once. I named him Rudán. Such a bright, happy child. Until his father got a hold of him. He became a warrior."

Amy thought about the baby she'd created. Would Emily have MacLir's mischievousness? Or her mother's relentless problem solving? Would they ever find the baby and the rest of their missing friends? Her mind snapped back to Brigit as the woman continued talking.

"Rudán fought and died in his father's war. They both died. The pain, at the time, was too much for me to bear. They say I created what is now called 'keening for the dead.' An anguished screech that could be heard all over the island. The pained scream of a mother learning of her son's death."

Taken aback, Amy didn't know what to say. She glanced at Brigit, who added, "I know Robin thinks of me as a sister, but I think of him as a son. They will regret what they have taken from me."

Still speechless, Amy nodded in agreement and Brigit gave a single slow regal nod in return.

Arriving in the infirmary, Amy was braced while carefully keeping her mind clear of emotion. Surface thoughts only, but ready for action. "So, did you like my idea about just picturing them here?"

"I said before. Simply believing they are here could cause them harm. We don't know what the magic would do to get them here."

"Then why did we come all this way?"

"For you to try scrying." Brigit pulled out a flat silver tray and set it on the table. She poured an inch of water into the tray and pushed it toward Amy. "This has gone too far. It's time to see what they're up to," mumbled Brigit.

"What do you mean?"

"Focus on the water. Pretend it's a window. You don't want to go there, and you don't want them here. You only want to look through the window and see if they are safe."

What if they are dead? Amy wanted to ask. Maybe she didn't want to see what had happened to them. In case thinking about them being dead hurt them somehow, she got a tighter rein on her worries.

Peering into the dish of water, she tried to imagine it was a window. Of course, it wasn't a window. It was simply water. She missed him, but how could water show her Robin? She still was not sure what love was, but if it existed, she loved Robin. For a chance to see him, she believed. Imagining the water as glass, when she focused on the edges of the dish, it took the shape of a window frame. If all she had to do was look through a window to make sure Robin was okay, she could do it.

She closed her eyes for a moment. Pictured his wavy hair and the single curl that fell onto his forehead. The cream-colored knit sweaters he always wore. His expressive green eyes. She peeked through the window, expecting to see him. And there he was.

"It worked!" Amy said.

"It worked too well," commented Brigit dryly.

The water had solidified into glass, pulling and stretching the shallow bowl into an actual window frame that sunk into Brigit's worktable. Secured in the wood like an actual window in a wall. On the other side of the glass was Robin in a blue bedroom, on a bed, asleep.

"He's so still," whispered Amy.

"But breathing," Brigit said reassuringly, a hand on Amy's shoulder. "Now, try finding Emily."

She remembered her first glimpse of the baby when Piper unwrapped the blanket to see a head covered in blonde fuzz. She peeked through the window, expecting to see the same baby. Emily was there! Safe and being bottle-fed by someone she could not quite see. Relief shot through her.

"Do you recognize either of these places?" Amy asked Brigit, who shook her head.

Sighing, Amy decided to look for MacLir. If anyone was dead, it was probably MacLir. Although she kept those thoughts as general as possible. She didn't want to accidentally believe him dead. Or, accidentally believe him alive into a zombie, if that was possible.

Pushing those concepts out of her mind, she pictured MacLir as she'd come to know him. A friendly bronze-tanned teen boy with kind aqua eyes. Robin had explained he was probably as old as the dawn of human ocean exploration. However, since he didn't appear old and didn't usually act mature, she'd come to think of him as a younger cousin, like

Piper, who was close to her age. Yet, watching MacLir and Piper together, they both seemed so freshly youthful.

She opened her eyes and leaned over the new window, expecting to see MacLir wherever he was, in whatever condition he was in. She was relieved to see he was in a bedroom too, a red-themed one, and he was alive. Unlike Robin, he was awake and enraged.

The bed had been replaced with a massive stone slab, and he was chained to it. Ankle, wrist, chest, and neck. Clearly, his captors were taking no chances he might be able to pull free and escape.

"Would you do me a favor? Can you search for Lucky?" Brigit asked, surprisingly timid. The shyness in her voice softened her usually stern presence.

Amy smiled. "Of course."

Lucky. A flashy man she'd only briefly seen in her vision of Brigit's baby. Although, once was enough to remember him. His black and jewel-toned clothes contrasted with his pale skin. His artful beard stubble and heavy arched eyebrows paired perfectly with his wavy dark hair. He was older, but in that dashingly mature way that made her mother swoon when flipping through glossy celebrity magazines.

It was not even certain Lucky had been captured. He might have lost his phone and not even known people wanted to talk to him. Same as MacLir, she carefully kept all expectations out of her mind. She believed she'd peek through the window and see Lucky no matter where he was or what he was doing.

Lucky was on the floor in a yellow bedroom, asleep but not alone. Two guards were beating him. It was shocking to see the violence after the last few relatively calm scenes in the various colored bedrooms. Lucky wasn't waking up. Maybe he was already knocked out? They wouldn't bother beating a dead man, so Amy took it as a hopeful sign.

When one of the men jumped on Lucky's arm, Amy's stomach flipped. Brigit made a strangled noise between a scream and sob, then rushed from the room.

Lucky

Everything hurt. Everything. Lucky tried to open his eyes, but his eyes hurt. No. Maybe just one of them? He cracked open one eye and saw pale yellow curtains. Brigit's infirmary was white, so he must be seeing colors wrong.

The infirmary was where he would be if he was in this much pain. Actually, he remembered being in the infirmary last. So, that made sense. What didn't make sense was the yellow curtains and how injured he was. He didn't remember an accident or a battle.

He closed his good eye again and assessed the damage. He'd been mortally wounded before, and none of his body felt that bad off. Bruised but not injured. Except for his arm. His arm was on fire. Probably broken. He wondered why Brigit had let him wake without dulling his pain first.

Lucky opened his good eye again, hoping to see Brigit's figure bustling around the room she knew so well. Instead, he found himself in quite a small bedroom. The yellow curtains were only the start. He also found yellow walls, carpet, and bedding. He was not a fan of yellow. So... not in the infirmary after all.

Again trying to recall what happened, he had a flash of memory. Visiting the infirmary... seeing Brigit... talking about... he could not remember what. Actually, maybe he imagined it, but he heard Brigit's voice now. On the other side of the door. Not the words, but her most angry, demanding, goddess-like tone. When she burst through the door, he smiled at her.

Trying to speak, he discovered his throat was too dry to properly make sound. "Hello," he weakly croaked.

"Hello," she replied, mirroring his smile, but her puffy eyes gave away her distress. Lucky again wondered what was going on.

He accepted a cup of water from Brigit and sipped it while she rambled. "He provided such hope at first. Hope for a return to our past glory. The hope was contagious among the High Court members. It started small. Helping him change a few laws. Adjusting a few beliefs, or looking the other way. I don't mind humans. But, if it's them or us, I choose us."

"I don't understand. What are you trying to say?"

"I miss my life. My castle. Sunlight. Midsummer festival celebrations that don't have to take place in a soggy forest. The old ways. Don't you miss anything from, well… from before the fall of our people?"

"I like things as they are now." He replied to her question, but his fuzzy brain was still trying to catch the thread of the conversation.

"Of course, you like things now," she scoffed. "You have a life outside the faerie mounds."

The bitterness in her voice registered as a thought struck his sluggish mind. "Do you want the old ways returned?" This conversation was trying to prod a memory from him. Like he'd had this conversation with Brigit before, but he was sure he hadn't.

The door burst open again. Ian and two guards appeared in front of his one good eye. "Well, they made quite a mess of you," the king commented mildly. "Sorry for that. It was necessary. I know how your power works. You can't shift away if you are in too much pain."

Lucky evaluated his injuries and realized the man was right. He was not in any danger of dying, but he was definitely in enough agony that flashing right now was not an option. The real question was, why did he need to flash away, and why was he being stopped from doing so?

"You didn't have to injure him to keep him here. He would have kept sleeping," shouted Brigit.

Shocked, Lucky glanced over at her. Brigit was soft-spoken and demure. Always. He'd never seen her shout. Or even emotional. He mentally smiled because that meant she must care about him to get this worked up.

"I had to wake him up. I couldn't talk to him if he was sleeping," said Ian.

His reasonable tone contrasted with Brigit's hysterical one as she said, "I've had enough. I'm healing Lucky and we're leaving. We'll take Robin, the baby, and MacLir on the way out too. I suspect they're here somewhere."

"I'll leave you two to talk for now, but I'll be back to speak with Lucky soon."

Brigit followed when he left the room, but the guards blocked her way. "You can't keep me here!" she called to him.

"I can and will," said Ian. "Also, if you heal his broken arm, we'll break it again. Over and over, again and again."

As Brigit paced and fumed at the foot of his bed, it finally hit Lucky that everything was not quite right. In fact, watching the relationship between her and Ian shatter, he remembered the conversation in the infirmity. She was Ian's ally. He remembered her telling him to sleep.

It was her fault he was here. Brigit had betrayed him, and now they were both prisoners.

CHAPTER 16

Ian

Ian sat in the best chair of the study and ground his teeth. It was his study now, but the bloodstain on the carpet continually reminded him this was not a place he'd built for himself. It was a throne he'd stolen. No, he told himself, not stolen, accepted. The same as his foster brother had assumed their father's throne on his death.

Although, that still bothered him. Why hadn't he been given their father's place to lead? He knew he'd been a disappointment at times, but they must trust him to lead. The plan his father developed clearly stated he was to rule as king in the faerie mounds, find the daughter of the sea, wipe out the humans, and guide their people to a new era above ground. Yet, how was he supposed to remain king of the faerie mounds if everyone was above ground? That next part of the plan was so unclear, but he was sure he'd get more directions soon.

Lucky was not part of his father's plan, however, Ian was sure that Lucky would agree to help once the plan was explained to him. The time had come to ask. To finally talk to Lucky, and Brigit had spoiled everything. He could have her removed from the room, but he knew enough about love to know it would upset Lucky. He'd have to talk to Lucky with Brigit in the room. Maybe if she understood the plan, she'd calm down too.

"Butler!" Ian called.

"Yes, sir?" The butler had appeared so quickly he must have been standing outside the door. Ian still had not learned his name, though he assumed the man had one.

"Bring tea to the yellow room. And, replace this rug."

"Yes, sir."

Practicing his words while going up the stairs, he took one deep breath outside the yellow room, then opened the door, waving at the guards to stay out in the hallway this time. Brigit had followed his orders. Lucky looked equally as awful as she looked mad.

In the heavy silence, he dragged a chair from the corner to the foot of the bed. While they continued to glare at him, he removed his hat.

Even though he was prepared for their shock, he was smug anyway. The first people in the mounds to know his secret. He was glad it was Lucky. His brother.

"Your hair—" gasped Brigit, putting a hand over her mouth.

"Yes," agreed Ian. His distinctive wavy blue-black hair was a perfect match for Lucky's own rare color. In fact, if he was not chubby, all their features would appear identical. He could see the connection dawning on them. See them evaluating their enemy anew. "I'm your brother, Lucky."

"How?" Lucky asked. "How did you survive being tossed in the water as a baby?"

"I was saved. By the sea dragon."

"Why weren't we raised together? How did you survive all these years outside the magical community?"

Ian wanted to reveal everything. How they had allies

sneaking out MacLir's immortal-giving ham to him and Tamlin, his foster brother. With only enough for two, his father had chosen his adopted apprentice and his son to have it. Instead, Ian kept to simple facts for now. "Father took me with him. To his new colony. We had important work to do."

Lucky's breath hitched, like a punch in the gut had removed all the air from his lungs. "Father? But he was killed too. When I—when we—were young."

"No," said Ian. Not ready to discuss their father, he steered the conversation back on track. "I am your brother. Look at my hair and eyes. Like Father's, like yours. You can't deny it."

"Well, no, I guess not, but," Lucky stammered. He was as speechless as Brigit.

Ian leaned forward, not quite pleading, and said, "I want us to be friends, Lucky. You're my brother." Ian smiled his charming smile, but didn't pour magic into it. He wanted to make a friend by choice this time. "Join me. Brigit has. She can heal you, and then we can change the world together."

"You have a funny way of being friendly," grumbled Lucky as he adjusted his broken arm. "I think Brigit is done following you, and holding me captive is an odd way to start a friendship."

"Not just a friendship—a partnership too. Hear me out." Lucky stared at Ian with one eye, the other grotesquely swollen shut. "Brigit, I can't talk to him while he looks so repulsive. Heal his face. Now and quickly." Brigit wrinkled her nose at the disrespectful order but moved her hands toward Lucky. As his brother relaxed, Ian added hastily, "Only his face."

Lucky

Lucky melted into the cool relief washing through him. The cut on his cheek knit back together, and the swelling around his eyes disappeared so he could use both of them. Even the non-visible bruises under his clothes eased and healed. The pain in his arm calmed to an almost manageable level. He'd been healed by Brigit many times and knew she could do more. Even before Ian objected, she'd stopped just short of healing him enough to flash. He wondered which side she was on.

"MacLir is the problem," Ian began. "He loves the humans, so he's keeping all the powerful men of our clans trapped. Living like rats in tunnels. He dragged us here and splintered our ways."

Lucky rolled his eyes. He'd heard all this before. Utter nonsense. The Tua De would have all died several millennia ago if not for MacLir's help. Or become workers for the humans that conquered them.

"MacLir banned our father from this island. Everything is MacLir's fault."

This new statement shook him. Could it be true? He'd always been told his father was killed. Not only killed, but murdered by his maternal grandfather. Lucky had executed the old man in revenge on a battlefield, as he'd been told to do by his uncle and The Voiceless Pure. Had he avenged the death of a father who lived, but chose to leave him behind?

Of all the people who said his father was dead, MacLir was never one of them. He'd never even implied it. Yet, he had not corrected Lucky's impressions either. Was it close enough to lying? Should he be angry with his foster father? He'd untangle that later. For now, he wanted to hear what other absurdity spouted from his newfound brother.

"Everything else is the fault of humans," Ian continued. "They tricked us into the dark. Because of MacLir, we can't live under the sun anymore. Because of humans, we can't go home."

Brigit sighed and pointed out, "Something is not quite right with your logic."

Ian ignored her. "The first step was to find the crow goddess. She still had enough allies here to get some of the High Court on our side. As required, she helped position me to begin infiltrating the court. It's probably a good thing that MacLir killed her before I could. I wish it had been at my own hands, but my allies would have been upset with me. Since MacLir did it, they were spurred to the ready even faster than planned."

Lucky remembered the falling out after the crow goddess had died last year. It was true that MacLir had killed her. He didn't know what Morgana had done to Ian, but on this point, they agreed. Lucky would have murdered the dark soul himself, given a chance. Apparently, revenge ran deep. It was all he'd known growing up. His uncle groomed him to avenge his father, win the war, and become king. So easily influenced when he was young. Like Ian.

The man in front of him, with eerily similar features—now that he was looking for them—was a pawn. Having been one himself, Lucky recognized the blind allegiance. The reckless rhetoric. He'd briefly been enthralled with The Voiceless Pure too. Until MacLir opened his eyes to the harm it was doing. MacLir was not the problem.

The Tua De lived in the elemental's realm because MacLir, an elemental, invited them, and they already trusted him. Lucky had been a child when MacLir had worked with the High Council to ban the leaders of the last group of Voiceless Pure from returning to Ireland. A punishment rarely handed down. However, the usually easy-going MacLir would not stand for the misuse of power or intolerance—and The Voiceless Pure stood for both.

Had his father been one of the banned leaders? Pieces he didn't know fit were clicking together, forming connections he would not be able to unlearn.

After pouring the tea brought in by a butler, Ian offered them some. Both he and Brigit shook their heads. Lucky had no intention of eating anything provided by this madman. After taking a few sips, Ian continued his boasting.

"I acted confused in the first battle. I let you think the Clock of Destiny had worked and removed our memories of the event. But, I shielded my followers. We lost the battle on purpose. You would never have won so easily. Three against my thirty. Ha! The cloak gave us an easy excuse to leave after I maimed the king. Also, it showed my followers how underhanded MacLir is. How he would use memory magic on sons of the pure. How many other times has he used it, and we don't remember?"

It was a good question, thought Lucky. Then he mentally shook himself, like a dog shaking off water. It was not a good question. MacLir didn't have a dishonest bone in his body, and he'd never heard the boy scheme or lie. His foster father was not going around erasing the memory of Tua De to keep them underground. He was sure of it.

Lucky steeled himself against other lies as Ian continued, "Our father created us for a purpose. You fulfilled your purpose by killing our grandfather and winning the first war. I am finally fulfilling my purpose to exterminate the humans for good. Humans will finally pay for their treachery."

"And after everyone is dead? What then?"

"Not everyone. Only the humans," said Ian, his eyes gleaming with anticipation.

An uneasy awareness crept through Lucky. He remembered Brigit saying MacLir and Robin were here too. Captured. He could push through the pain eventually and escape, but this might be his one chance to learn as much as possible. "So, all the humans are gone. What then?"

"Well, utopia," said Ian confidently, with a shrug. "A return to the old ways."

"How, with no humans? The old ways, and even the new ways, require servants."

"Yes, many Tua De will be pressed into service to assist the High Court."

"You promised them the High Court won't exist," interrupted Brigit.

"So? They won't know until it's too late for them. Why does the working-class matter anyway? It's their role in life to serve."

"Is it?"

Ian ignored this question and continued laying out his plans. His plea for an understanding that Lucky would never agree with. After another minute of rantings and ramblings, Lucky cut him off by turning to Brigit. "Please tell me he messed with your mind and pushed you into helping him."

Brigit stared at the thick yellow carpet, an attractive pink flush creeping up her cheeks. "No. He tried to subtly influence my mind. It was cute. His powers, like yours, are no match for me. However, I wanted to believe. If not in Ian, then in the change he was bringing. I didn't know most of what he just told us, and I don't agree with everything they do. But, Lucky, even you have to agree. Our living conditions must change."

Before Lucky could reply to Brigit, Ian began a frenzied fuming speech. They had him focused on what he'd been taught, and now the hatred was pouring out of him. "The problem is the half-magics. Taking all our food and space. They will go right along with the humans."

"Go where?" Lucky asked. "What is the goal here?"

"Humans will all die. All of them. Even the half-humans. We'll be soaking the globe in blood magic to kill them all. Only the pure will remain."

This was the most shocking of all the revelations Ian had announced so far. After years of mixing with the island natives, few pure Tua De remained. Including himself and his brother. "You fool. You are half-human. You'll die too."

"Lies," Ian hissed. "Our father was as pure as the first wanderers."

"But our mother was human."

"I… I don't believe you," said Ian, his initial shock fading back to furious anger. "Father would not have lied about that. You are trying to save your human friends, and it won't work. We'll be even stronger without humans. I'll finish my task, and when you are free again, you'll see how much better life is. You'll agree with me, and we'll be friends."

"Never," said Lucky.

Ian stood so quickly that his chair toppled over. He glared at Lucky, then stalked from the room, shouting, "We are changing our future!"

CHAPTER 17

Piper

"Brigit left me on my own in the empty infirmary, with no way to contact anyone and too scared to leave on my own."

That didn't seem like Brigit, but why would Amy lie? "So, you were in the infirmary this whole time? I was worried you were captured too." Piper collapsed onto the ship bench, relieved she wasn't alone anymore. She'd considered going to get Clara, just to have company. She couldn't rescue everyone by herself. Her hope was dissolving fast, and even the comfort of having Amy back was not helping much.

"I have terrible news." Amy's words sliced through that fragile hope. A million things that could have gone wrong bloomed in Piper's imagination. What if MacLir was dead? She didn't want to know, but waited for Amy to continue. "Ian is planning to kill all the humans in one strike, using magic. Even the half-humans."

In the long list of her fears, this was one she had never considered. Piper knew some of the Tua De wanted to kill some humans in war, but this was so much worse. She pulled Wave Sweeper's key from her pocket and flipped the worry stone between her fingers instead of rubbing it. A sure sign she was more agitated than she realized. "How do you know all this?"

"The head cook told me."

"How does Ginger know?"

"Brigit came to her in a dream and told her. She requested Ginger get me out of the mounds and back to you."

Piper's mind was reeling, never expecting the recent evil chatter in the mounds to actually happen. She had firmly believed in MacLir's strength to keep everything peaceful. Now he was gone, and she was alone. She never planned to do anything alone ever again. Now, not only did she have to rescue him, she had to save every human on the planet? If she and Amy didn't, who would? "But why did Brigit send Ginger? Where is Brigit?"

"Captured."

"Great. Just great." Piper's stomach dropped. She tried to list who was left to help. Herself, Amy, and perhaps Ginger. All the other Tua De she'd met were missing. "We are running out of allies."

"You have me," said a child-like voice from the water.

"Fia!" Piper could hear the relief in her voice, glad she was not entirely without friends.

Amy joined Piper at the ship's edge, saying, "Oh! Ginger also said Ian is Lucky's brother. Long believed dead, but rescued by a sea dragon. Is there more than one sea dragon?"

"Only me in the human realm," said Fia.

"How did you rescue Ian?"

"A goodly phrased question. I can answer. On a dark night, in a choppy sea, babies were dropped in the water from a high tower. Half Tua babies. All of them. MacLir helped the shifters use their magic to live in the water, but three were not born with the same ability as the other shapeshifters. MacLir grabbed one above me. I grabbed a second in my mouth. The third dropped, no one to catch him," said Fia sadly. Their head wove back and forth with the memory of past distress. "I only have one mouth. Could only save one."

"Where did the baby grow up?" Amy asked curiously.

"Another ideal question. Good, good. He lived with his father, in the second Tua community. A pure community. They don't mix with the humans." Fia's voice dropped, and in a tone showing the sea dragon didn't approve, said, "They still do blood magic. With babies."

Fear sent tingles skittering across Piper's back and along her arms. Blood magic with babies… and they'd stolen her child. Besides, MacLir had never told her about a second community. Did he even know? "Why didn't you tell us this before?"

"You didn't ask the right questions before."

"Is my baby at the new community?"

"No, no," said Fia, the big head shaking side to side, droopy whiskers flinging water onto the deck.

Frustrated, Piper stomped a foot. This whole conversation had been pointless. "Fia, will you help us find MacLir and my baby?"

"I can't. You won't need me anyway."

"We do need you," said Piper. She was stronger with MacLir. They made a good pair. If he was by her side again, they could fix this. She was sure of it. "Help us find the god of the sea. Please."

"I can't. I will. I can't. Half measures," the dragon mumbled. Finally, Fia said clearly, "Find Odin."

Piper sighed. "You've been acting strange lately. Stranger than normal." Fia huffed and slipped into the water before Piper could ask any other questions.

It was too much. So much hope had soothed her when Fia appeared that watching the dragon leave pulled Piper to the depths of despair. How could she and Amy fight a whole civilization to get back the boy she loved? It was impossible. Impossible.

Her vision tilted as her head went light. Sweat popped out on her whole body. The sun, warm and comforting a moment ago, was too hot now, burning her bare arms. She pulled down her scrunched-up sleeves to her hands, but the fabric was rough on her suddenly overly sensitive skin. Tears trickled down her cheeks, landing in her mouth and the salty taste made her queasy. Her throat was closing up. She could not get a full breath. She didn't care. Nothing mattered. Everything was hopeless. Impossible to fix.

Amy

"Piper!" said Amy anxiously as the girl collapsed in tears and balled up in the corner where the cabin met the railing. Piper's eyes squeezed shut, and her tears made puddles on the polished deck. Amy had seen Clara overwhelmed like this, so she knew better than to touch Piper right now.

Quickly darting away to the bathroom sink, Amy returned with a glass of water and sat nearby. In arm's reach, but giving Piper plenty of space. In a calm voice, she said, "Piper, try to hear my voice."

The girl didn't respond, but Amy continued, speaking normally but keeping her voice quiet and clear. "I didn't have a chance to say it yet. Brigit showed me how to scry, and we checked on everyone. They are alive." Amy mentally facepalmed for forgetting to tell Piper about MacLir. She'd only delivered the worst news with no hope, but now a path forward had unfolded with the sea dragon's suggestion. Piper's eyes popped open, unfocused, but Amy took it as a good sign, so she continued, "Odin must be the key."

After a few moments of holding still, Piper sat up, sitting cross-legged, her back leaning on the cabin for support. Still not speaking, she pulled out her worry stone and flicked it between her fingers at a frantic pace. Tears still streamed, soaking into her wet shirt, but Amy watched as some of Piper's disorientation visibly receded.

Amy pushed the glass of water closer to Piper, and after she'd sipped some, her new friend was able to whisper, "You saw MacLir? He's alive?"

"Yes. So, now we need to listen to the sea dragon and find Odin."

"I saw Odin once," said Piper, her voice stronger, but still speaking slowly. "I saw him through someone else's eyes—long story—but I think Lucky met him in Sweden. At a dock, in a small bay. Somewhere with lots of red roofs. How would we find that?"

"Um," said Amy, stalling for time while she quickly flipped through everyone she'd met in the magical community. Piper was not wrong to panic. They were low on people to call for assistance. Amy blushed as she remembered the helpful naked selkie man stretched out next to her on the island beach. "The selkies! They might know."

"The selkie's roam," said Piper, shaking her head. "We could search the whole coastline and might never find them."

They both sat lost in the thought, and Flutter strolled out of the cabin. The gray kitten stretched its front legs, then its wings, yawning wide. She settled in Piper's lap to start an elaborate bath.

As Piper stroked the fluffy fur, her breathing finally became normal. Amy didn't know what to say, so she left Piper alone to continue staring blankly at the shimmery sails flapping in the breeze. The blue and green fabric shades complimented both each other and the emerald and sapphire gemstones sparkling around the dragon-shaped figurehead.

Watching Piper's panic had melted the last of Amy's anger about the situation. Anger was pointless. In fact, everything was pointless. Why had she gone traveling? Was this her fault? No, she'd fallen into it. Because Robin was a spy. Maybe he would always have been captured. MacLir too.

Nothing they did, and nowhere they searched, was helping. So why bother doing anything if nothing mattered? They'd all be dead in a hundred years, and none of this would matter. Well, not the immortals, but she'd be dead. Probably. Unless she too became immortal as goddess? MacLir had implied as much, but now he was gone. And Robin was gone. This was all too much for her brain to take. It swirled in circles with information she didn't want to process.

When Piper's eyes narrowed, Amy desperately wanted to ask what she was thinking, but held still. When Piper's finger started flipping her worry stone again, Amy wondered if Piper was getting re-agitated. Should she say something comforting?

Finally, Piper focused on her and said, "So, you learned to scry in the Otherworld, right?"

Amy nodded.

"Which is kind of like visions?"

"Sort of," agreed Amy.

"It's your power of belief letting you do that, because the Otherworld has more magic. Magic is more flexible there, but Earth has magic too. Not as much, but you can see visions here as a goddess. So, you should be able to scry visions here, right?"

Amy considered the possibility of magic in the human realm. She did see visions here, but had not considered them as similar to her unpredictable power in the faerie mounds. She remembered how realistic the window was, as if she was peeking into someone's house. Unlike her visions, which were similar to a dream or a memory, only in her mind.

"Scrying is traditional magic," Piper pointed out. "It's said even humans can do it. Witches are probably people like you, with strong opinions and beliefs. Your belief magic has probably been helping you your whole life, and you didn't realize it. I bet if you tried to scry right now, it would work."

Excitement rose in Amy's chest. Her gut was telling her Piper was correct. "What would I try to see?"

"The selkies. We might have better luck figuring out the location of a selkie based on their surroundings. Seeing Odin with more red roofs won't help us at all."

After moving the ship to land, so the scrying bowl didn't slosh, Piper led Amy to the kitchen in her room. Amy marveled at the little apartment Piper lived in. She'd seen both the blue and green guest rooms, and the bathroom, of course, but had never been in the space MacLir and Piper shared.

Past a hallway with a door to their private bath, the room opened up to hold a massive canopy bed draped in the same sparkling fabric as the ship's sails. The kitchen along one long wall was well stocked with plenty of counter space. Piper pulled a round cake pan out of a cupboard and poured water into it. Placing it next to the sink, she asked, "Will this work?"

Amy nodded and stared into the water. She pictured the selkie who had saved her. He'd pushed her onto the beach, then joined them briefly, changing from seal to human. She pictured what she could remember of his features, and his voice as he demanded an apology kiss. She believed the water would show her this person.

The water went cloudy, white as milk. Next, color bloomed on the surface. A beach below cliffs. The view zoomed in slowly on the seals lying on the beach and two figures walking toward them. With a start, Amy recognized herself and Piper. One seal shimmered into a human and stood to greet them. The vision paused on their faces, showing them with the first selkie she'd met. Then the water went clear again.

Confused at what the vision meant, Amy asked Piper. "Could you see it too?"

"Yes! Even better, I know that beach. Let's go!"

"Wait, wait," said Amy. "Did you see we were talking to him? That didn't happen in my past, and it can't be happening right now. I think my visions in the mound were what was happening at that very moment."

Piper shrugged. "Must be the future," she said dismissively. "It's how your other visions work, seeing the future. Maybe the magic got mixed. Either way, we know where to go." She rushed out to the bench and got the ship in the air.

Amy followed more slowly, her steps faltering as the ship took off, faster than Piper usually flew. Somehow she'd managed to scry the future. She already saw the future for women she'd read, so why was it surprising that Piper's idea worked? She didn't know why shock still flowed through her, but it left her shaken.

For so many years, she knew who she was. What she wanted from life. But now? Was there even a name for what these discoveries made her? A witch? A goddess? These titles didn't fit the country girl she was or the strange new person she'd become lately.

"Amy! Come on!" Piper shouted.

She discovered she was standing in the hallway, staring into space, and the ship had stopped moving. As she stepped out of the cabin into the sunshine to follow Piper, one last thought drifted through her mind. That this wild, magical year continued to change her life and she was excited to see where it led her next.

CHAPTER 18

Piper

"Can I get you anything?" Piper asked. A shirt, some pants, or a blanket, she wanted to add.

The female selkie gave Piper a knowing grin and replied, "No, thank you, I'm fine."

The selkie had waved away an offer of the bench, in favor of sitting leaned against the edge of the ship near the ladder, with her knees to her chest and her arms comfortably wrapped around her shins. Her long thick black hair flowed around her pale skin.

"She smells of fish, but does not have any with her," sent Flutter, still hopefully sniffing the hands and hair of the new arrival. The kitten's ears were semi-flattened, and her back slightly arched. Curious, but ready to run.

Piper didn't reply to either of them. Purposefully shifting her eyes away, she caught Amy also staring at their passenger.

"Let me know when we're past Denmark. I can direct you from there," added the seal-turned-woman.

Piper briefly cut her eyes toward the figure and nodded. She wanted to act okay with a naked woman on her deck, but the woman's calm boldness was making her feel too much. Alarmed. Anxious. Attracted. She stopped her thoughts before they could launch into an alphabetical list of emotions starting with B words next.

Instead, she focused on Wave Sweeper's key in her hand and reached for the ship, similar to how she stretched her senses out for the visions of someone's future. The ship responded, lifting high in the air and zipping toward their destination. Toward an answer to their problems. A new ally.

It was good to have confirmation the selkies were willing allies. They'd spoken with the one Amy knew, and he'd pointed them in the direction of their new ship guest. She said she often visited Odin and would gladly show them the way.

Piper would usually have preferred directions instead of a physical guide, but time was important now, so it was worth being uncomfortable with another person on board, for the mental comfort of knowing they were going to the correct village.

With their guide's directions, the fishing port soon came into view, familiar from her one memory of it. She dropped the ship into the water and steered it in, holding it steady as the others descended the ladder and tied it to the dock. "What now?"

"Follow the main road until you see a cafe with a large sign for waffles. Odin likes waffles. Go inside and think hard about Odin. Rather like a prayer. If he's not busy, he'll be along shortly." She gave a cheerful wave and dove into the ocean.

Amy and Piper's eyes met in shock, but Piper quickly glanced away. With nothing to do or say except follow the instructions, they found the main street and the cafe, then ordered waffles for three.

Piper had never prayed to any god before. She pictured the man she'd briefly seen. Standing on the dock in long robes of gray, the rest of him all shades of gray, and she began to pray. Dear Odin, you don't know me, but I'm a friend of Lucky and MacLir. I am waiting at your waffle cafe and have ordered you a waffle. Please drop by for lunch as soon as you can. It's very important.

She thought the message. Really hard. Twice. Wondering if there were special words to end prayers for mythological gods. After a year of being a goddess, there was still much for her to learn about their world. She wondered if people could pray to her. If they did, how would she know? She dismissed the random thought when she saw Odin meandering toward their table.

Amy

Amy was deep in prayer to an unknown god. She didn't know what to picture in her mind since she'd never seen Odin, but she sent her plea flinging outward. Imagining it as a paper airplane on the wind currents, sprinkling her words to every town and forest in the country. Odin, mighty god of war, please accept this offering of a waffle. We are in dire need of your urgent help.

"You bought me a waffle? How kind." The man who dropped into the empty chair at their table was not what Amy expected. He was old and gray. Weather-aged skin and gray all over, from the tip of his hat to the toes of his boots. He smiled kindly at the pair of girls and dragged the waffle toward himself. Pulling a little flask from a pocket, he opened it and poured honey over the waffle.

"So, what can I do for you two on this lovely day?" When neither of them spoke, he took a bite of his dessert and waited patiently.

Amy spoke first. "My name is Amy, and I'm the new Goddess of Creativity. Piper's child was stolen by someone in the faerie mounds. We think it might be the new king."

"He's captured MacLir too! And Lucky. And Brigit," cut in Piper.

"Right," agreed Amy, "and Robin, along with most of MacLir's allies living in the mounds. He's holding them captive somewhere to keep them from stopping his plans of spreading magic to kill all the humans."

"Hmm. A sad tale, to be sure," said Odin. "But why are you here?"

"For you!" Piper exclaimed.

"For your help," Amy clarified. "We have no one else to turn to."

Odin shook his head. "It's not my fight."

Piper's breathing quickened as she began to rock in her seat. "But, but… you're the god of war."

"So?"

"This is a war!"

"Not my war. Let me tell you a little story." Odin ate the last bite of his waffle and settled back in his seat. "Long ago, in an age of heroes, when I was a much younger man, the Tuatha Dé Danann appeared in Ireland. They instantly clashed with the locals, battling with invincible magical weapons to take over the island. For decades the natives fought and lost, but for one hold out. Balor was a king determined not to lose.

"A prophecy was floated around saying he would be killed by his own grandson. He only had one daughter, so he locked her in a tower and refused to let her see any men. He filled the tower with over six hundred women, a feat in those days. The women were scattered on every level of the tower to stop any man from reaching the top.

"Secure in the knowledge he'd changed his destiny, Balor began the war to take back the island. He didn't know his enemies knew the location of the tower. Cian, a young Tua

De charmer deep in the war efforts, went to the castle to create a son for his cause. A son with Balor's daughter to fulfill the prophecy.

"On each level of the tower, the handmaidens succumbed to Cian's charm and let him pass after a romp with him. By the time Cian left the tower, every single woman was pregnant. Balor checked on his daughter a year later and found her surrounded by children. Worried that one might be his grandson from the prophecy, he tried to kill them all by tossing them out of the tower into the ocean below.

"The six hundred handmaiden's babies shifted to seal form with the help of the sea god, becoming selkies with the sheen of Cian's blue-black hair. Balor's daughter had triplets, but they were born without the ability to shapeshift, so MacLir was only able to save one. He was named Lugh and put in the care of an uncle. Lugh's birth was mixed up in hostility on both sides. MacLir didn't like what the boy's head was being filled with. Revenge, hate, and excitement for battle. After the war, he took Lugh under his wing, helped him let go of his magical weapons and taught him how to live in peace. They've been inseparable ever since.

"The Tua De didn't rule long, comparatively. They were conquered by the next invaders, but Lucky's ancestors were aggressive and bloodthirsty, even before they were tricked underground. All that anger bubbling under the surface is finally coming to a head. Nothing anyone can do to stop the fight now. It was always inevitable."

Her waffle was forgotten and shoulders drooped more with every word when Piper asked, "You were our last hope, but you really think nothing can stop this?"

Piper didn't seem ready to quit and Amy was not either. If Odin himself refused to help, if he was not the answer, maybe the answer was in his story? She reviewed everything she knew so far. The captives, mostly sleeping or chained. The story Odin told about Lucky. Then she remembered that Lucky had not been bound in her scrying vision. Maybe it was only for the beating they were giving him, but they might not tie him up again if he was in bad shape.

"Odin, you said they had magical weapons. Are those still around somewhere?" Amy asked.

"Oh definitely, hard to destroy magical weapons," he replied with a chuckle.

"Can you tell me about one of them? One that Lucky had?"

Odin described his favorite of Lucky's weapons. Not one Lucky made, but much older than either of them. A spear that was undefeatable. He almost lovingly described the handle and the tip, the design, and its weight. His description was so detailed that Amy could practically see it.

She paired the description with the image of Lucky in the yellow room and pushed. She didn't know if her belief magic would work in the human realm, but she believed in Piper's belief. It had worked for scrying and she was getting desperate.

Ian

Having the hat off was a relief. He imagined the tight interior band had started to constrict his ability to think. Now he was thinking hard and could not stop.

Everything was going smoothly, and it was all his doing. He was an amazing leader. He always knew he could be. So, why had Tamlin been brought it as father's heir? Some scrawny child, chosen from the populace and raised as his younger brother to steal Ian's rightful place as leader. The idea was absurd.

A wave of jealousy swooped in, it always did, but Ian didn't hide it this time. At this moment, it shifted from envy to rightful anger. His father should have chosen him as the next leader instead of Tamlin. Ian was old, much older than Tamlin. He'd done everything his father asked and had still been replaced.

Well, if his father was watching from somewhere in the realms of the dead, he'd see what a mistake he made. Because Ian was an excellent ruler. The upcoming ceremony would prove he could follow the plan and guide their people to victory over MacLir and the humans. A new age would begin for the elite of his people.

He picked up the newspaper off his desk and smiled at the headlines. The whole front page was full of all the contradicting information Ian had fed them. Based on all the lies he'd told the working poor. It was almost comical how they believed him.

They all pictured themselves as rulers in the new era, but not everyone could rule. Most people would be forced to labor for their betters. When the humans were gone, the ordinary among them would be the next workers and have no choice in their drudgery.

Let them dream for now, though. Let them all believe in a better future until he could make it happen for some. When the new future was formed, he would rule. Even over Tamlin. Or would he?

The confusion over this part of the plan still bothered him. Who was in charge? His father's old generals had set everything in motion at the appointed time, foretold by the ancient seer, but had been vague about what would happen. They had put his brother in charge of the elite of his home clan and sent him here to clear the way for an above-ground golden era.

They had heavily implied he would be High King, but clearing the way didn't exactly mean he would rule. Not if he examined their exact words.

A tiny suspicion snaked through his chest. Lucky had said he was half-human. Would his father send him here to die in the ceremony Ian was commanded to preside over? No. His father could not be so cruel to a son returned to him. Ian would not believe it. Lucky was simply misinformed.

However, even with Lucky's delusions, his long-lost brother could still be helpful. If Tamlin and his generals arrived and tried to take Ian's place as High King, he would need powerful allies. He and his warrior brother, his real brother, commanded similar magic skills. Together they would be unstoppable. It was worth trying one more time before he left for the ceremony.

CHAPTER 19

Lucky

"I'm going to give you one more chance, since maybe you still don't fully understand," announced Ian as he entered the room. The door slammed into the wall, and two guards entered with him.

Lucky had jumped in surprise. Uncommon for him, but he was on edge with his broken arm. The motion had jarred his arm, and fresh waves of pain brought tears to the corners of his eyes.

He refused to let them fall, though. He was ashamed to admit, only to himself, that he'd gone a little soft in this era of no battles and nearly no pain. Even minor scratches were soothed away by Brigit's healing powers. Brigit, who had betrayed him and everyone he knew.

Through his haze of pain, he tried to focus his meandering thoughts on the new king. The man standing in front of him. His brother with the plans of a madman.

Ian kicked away the chair he'd sat in last time, gripped the bed's footboard with both hands, and leaned forward, staring into Lucky's eyes. "You love Brigit. I know you do.

I've seen how much she loves you. Brigit understands the needs of our people, and you should trust her."

Lucky cut his eyes at Brigit, but she was pointedly examining the yellow carpet. Her head tilted away from him, hiding most of her face. If she knew this was the right course to take, the right way to move forward, why wasn't she as fervent as Ian? Where was her agreement?

"The Milesians tricked us." Ian's voice rose. "You were there, you know what happened. They gave us the option to join them or control half of Ireland, then they herded our people underground and planned to keep us there. It's degrading. Infuriating."

Lucky decided now was not a good time to point out that MacLir had been the one to save them during the Tua De's darkest hour. Guiding them through the cave openings to the Otherworld, where the defeated people could build a new life under Ireland's green hills.

His cheek quirked with the need to smile at Ian's implication he had lived through it. Although Lucky had not lived it either, since MacLir had already made him immortal. Already living partly in the Otherworld, Lucky was not one of those defeated in the war with the Milasians and tricked underground. He was not one of the conquered miserable people that had no way to restore their sense of worth and clan loyalties. His smile was because Ian had not been there either. Lucky still didn't know where his brother had been hiding, but it was not on this island.

"Clearly, humans are the problem. They were what our ancestors, our own father, fought against to maintain leadership. They are the cause of our downfall and despair. They are a burden to the land they live on. An infection causing the natural world around them to die."

Lucky considered pointing out their people had not treated the land much better, but instead let Ian continue his ranting without interruption. He was clearly angry, and nothing Lucky said would quiet this rage. He'd seen it before, in the old ones.

"I've already found a baby to use. Human, but with non-Tua magic. The blood ritual was worked out by our father and other clan leaders. The magic will spread to the whole earth, instantly killing humans and half-magics. We'll be all that's left, so we can return to the surface. Return to our rightful rule of this strong magical island."

Lucky had never heard anything so foolish. He finally broke his silence to ask, "Why are you telling me all this?"

"So you know. I want you to understand what we are working toward. Of course, I'll be the High King, but you could lead too. As a clan king, or by my side as one of my generals."

The hope in Ian's voice pulled at Lucky. He'd never had a close bond with anyone except MacLir. Not even his wives had truly known him. They only liked his position as king. He was hoping for something more with Brigit. As Ian was clearly hoping for something more from him. To have a brother would be a gift he could have treasured.

However, someone had twisted Ian's mind, similar to how he'd been given spun truth and lies together as a young boy. Ian had not had MacLir as a role model. Someone who had snapped Lucky out of what otherwise would have been complete brainwashing.

Pity for Ian didn't excuse his brother's current or future actions, but it laced through his next comment. "I can't participate," said Lucky, shaking his head slowly and showing his sadness. It was the only balm he could offer Ian, since agreement was not possible and friendship seemed hopeless. "I understand the plan, but I cannot help you with it."

Ian straightened, and the pleading in his eyes shifted to a glare.

"I'm going to give you one more chance," said Lucky, "since maybe you still don't fully understand." Ian recognized his own words from moments earlier, and his shoulders stiffened as his body tensed. Clearly, he'd taken the phrase as a mocking insult, but now Lucky had his attention. "You are half human."

The two guards at the door exchanged glances, and it was clear they were thinking about what this news could change if others knew it. A half-magic was rarely allowed as High King, but never in the Pure. If Ian was not a full elite, he would immediately be stripped of the title. Lucky didn't have time to think about anyone except Ian right now.

"You are right about our father. He fought the humans. He was born from one of the first Tua De to arrive on this island. He didn't love our human mother. We were created as part of the effort to have an advantage in the war, and it worked. It's true I did what I was told, and the war ended, but maybe the plan was wrong. Maybe this plan is wrong too."

Ian was shaking his head. A flash of disbelief was replaced by white-hot anger. "You are lying. You are trying to slander me to save the humans, but it won't work. I'm the king now. I will lead our people back to the golden era, and there is nothing you can do to stop me."

When Ian tried to leave in a huff, he was confronted with the guards' narrowed, calculating eyes and tight lips. They had heard the truth in Lucky's words and clearly wondered what side they should be on.

"You two, stay in this room to guard the dangerous friend of MacLir. He is no friend to your king and our people. He will try to stop us if he can," said Ian. Pinning Lucky with one last glare, he shouted, "We'll be even stronger without humans. We are changing our future!"

When the door shut behind him, Lucky slumped into the bed, discovering how tense his shoulders had become while arguing. Ian was in as much danger as Lucky from this crazy scheme. "Is he really so inept and delusional? He must be playing a part."

"He truly believes it," said Brigit.

Lucky almost jumped at her words. She'd been quiet since the last time Ian had left, and kept silent through their exchange of words this time. When had he become so skittish?

His nerves could not take much more of sitting here helpless. Ian's comment had got him thinking. What could he do to stop the plan? "He's dopey and dumb. How is he coordinating people to follow him?"

"None of it is his doing. Supporters are doing the real work, and he's a popular figurehead. Everything has gotten out of hand, and I had no idea about the plan to kill, well, everyone. I've been so stupid. Can you forgive me?"

Lucky remembered his time being manipulated by the Voiceless Pure. Murdering humans. Killing his own grandfather on the battlefield. It had seemed so right at the time and yet so wrong now, with more life experience.

He realized he'd been allowed to live among the humans, adopt their clothes and some of their habits. Meanwhile, Brigit had been stuck here, underground, away from most humans by the High Court's rules. Only allowed above the surfaces for brief seasonal festivals. Even then, humans were not part of the celebrations unless they wandered in accidentally and became followers or servants of the faeries.

Humans were complicated, but life would be so dull without them. He had come around to liking them, and maybe Brigit could too. For now, she was upset over her role in this mess, and that he could understand. Even forgive.

Reaching awkwardly with his good hand, he patted her knee. She finally looked at him, and the grief in Brigit's eyes was something he recognized. "Good and evil don't exist, Brigit. People always have reasons for their actions. Even if not everyone agrees on the same reasons or the same actions."

Brigit nodded, tears streaming down her face, so Lucky continued. "You did what you believed was right. I can respect your boldness, if not your methods. I forgive you. Now though, we are on the same team. So, we can make a difference together. Right?"

He could not think of a time he'd seen Brigit cry. He could not remember a time he'd been so jumpy either. They were both not at their best, but they had to do something if everyone was captured and stuck.

As he pushed his mind past the pain to work out an escape, something heavy leaned against his arm. Glancing over, he barely kept himself from jerking in surprise when he saw his invincible spear. Not just one of his famous weapons, but the most magical and terrifying of them all. A weapon he'd acquired as king, but was never sure its past stories were real. Allegedly it had been brought to Ireland by the old ones. A weapon created long before he was born and meant for vicious battle.

A dangerous weapon, with a mind of its own. People called it bloodthirsty, and they were close to correct. The tip, made of a metal he'd never been able to identify, was soaked in battle magic and drawn toward blood, except for the person holding it. Even now, he felt it shifting, slowly reorienting to point at his leg. He grasped it quickly, and it stopped. Only briefly. It straightened out to point directly at one of the guards across the room.

The guards didn't notice the motion, but when Brigit did she raised an eyebrow at Lucky and put a hand on his shoulder. Pretending to continue their conversation as if nothing had happened, her voice was calmer than the shock in her eyes. "Thank you for understanding. We can make a difference to our people. I'll do anything to prove I'm on your side now."

Comforting relief from pain washed through Lucky. The bones in his arm knitted together, and the rest of his bruises healed. His arm was still weak and would take time to finish recovering naturally, but it would no longer hold him back from flashing. Brigit poured energy into him. So much energy. He felt like he could take on the world. Or at least confront the guards.

One of the guards finally caught on as the healing was completed, but it was too late. Lucky grasped the spear tighter and believed he was standing next to the guard. He disappeared from the bed, reappearing next to the more alert guard.

His spear sprang forward, almost on its own. Singing triumphantly in an impression only Lucky could sense as the wielder, the spear buried deep into the other man's leg. As the guard screamed in pain and fell, he tried to lash out with his sword, but Lucky dodged.

At first, slow to respond, the other guard jumped into the fight with a direct hit to Lucky's upper arm. A swing that might have taken off his whole arm only managed to cut it deeply as Lucky flashed and reappeared two feet away. He tried to stab this man in the thigh too, incapacitating instead of killing, but his spear jerked at the last moment and went directly into the guard's chest. Slicing through armor like it was butter, the savage spear tip punctured his lung and came out the other side.

Lucky held tight to the spear and backed away, removing the weapon and shaking his head, annoyed. Back in the mists of his history, this was once his favorite weapon. They'd been attuned to each other with a shared purpose. Kill, and kill some more, for the glory of the Tuatha Dé Danann. Now though, it was a struggle to keep the spear under his control.

He'd locked the spear in a box filled with special sand magicked to keep the spear calm. He couldn't even guess how it had managed to wake from the sand, escape from the box, and appear in his bed. He was glad to have a weapon, though.

Brigit shook her head at the dead guard, at one of their people beyond her skill to heal, but her smile at Lucky showed she didn't blame him. She knew the old weapon he carried. Death followed in its wake, always.

Putting a hand over Lucky's wound, she repaired it, then pointed to the guard. "I'm going to heal him too, but in case someone else needs me more, I won't fatigue myself," she assured Lucky. He loved that leaving anyone in pain was not Brigit's way, and he smiled as he watched her kneel next to the guard who was still alive. Putting her hand over his head, she said, "SLEEP." He instantly went limp, and the damage to his leg knitted together enough to stop the bleeding.

Lucky nodded and gave her a hand up. She was so close. Her scent mixing with the triumph of battle made Lucky lightheaded. He knew they needed to hurry. To escape. To rescue anyone they could on the way. However, she was so near that he found he could not move. Her hand was still in his, and she wasn't pulling away either.

He remembered the kiss on the dock. He was sure the quick kiss had been a promise of a possible future. She'd kissed him first, and he'd wanted to do it again ever since. Now or never, he decided.

Leaning slightly in, their lips met. Rather than the brief flirty graze of contact last time, this kiss deepened, and he pulled her close as the room around them and his goals faded from his mind. Only she was real. An anchor for his long life that had recently seemed adrift in too much time. Too long a life lived. If he could be with her, he could live again.

He would have held her close and continued for eternity, but she pulled away. "We need to go."

Lucky nodded, wishing for more time and a different situation. He kept hold of Brigit's hand and kicked open the door. She chuckled at his antics, but he felt as invincible as his spear and was planning to enjoy it.

CHAPTER 20

Piper

So, Odin was not the savior they needed. Now what? He'd kindly escorted them back to the ship, but refused to go with them.

Piper's stomach churned with the threat of another panic attack.

Amy, quiet since the restaurant, cleared her throat to get everyone's attention. "I know you won't go with us, but would you grant us one favor if you don't have to leave the dock?"

"Perhaps."

"Help us get to the other realm, where my magic is stronger. We can't get there on our own."

"Why would you want to go there? You'd be stuck."

"I can scry from the human side, but it only shows snippets of the future. My scrying is much more powerful in the faerie realm."

"More than fairies live there," Odin grumbled, but continued. "Everyone get aboard the ship. You too, ya slippery heap o' blubber. I know you're sneaking around down there."

The seal lept from the water and plopped onto the low wooden dock. She shape-shifted into their nude guide with a big grin.

Piper had never before considered how other gods accessed the magical realm. All the past times MacLir had pulled them into the Otherworld, he did it simply by thinking about it. Of course, as guardian of the realm, he was tied more closely to it.

When everyone was on deck, Odin waved his hand in a complex pattern The shape he drew glowed faintly in the air for a moment, and as it faded away, the dock and the town disappeared around them. Pristine wild forest surrounded them, without a single human to build and reshape it. Coastal conifers huddled so tightly together she could hardly see between them as they crowded right up to the rocky shoreline.

Piper considered leading everyone to the spot where they were scrying last time, but hesitated. Inviting Amy into her private space had been simple, but she didn't want all these people trooping into her bedroom. Gripping her worry stone, she moved Wave Sweeper to a flat part of the shore, made sure the ship was steady, and told everyone to wait.

Grabbing the still drying cake pan from the dish rack, she hesitated again. Emotions weighed her, and she tried to pick out what exactly was wrong, but everything was wrong. It was all too much. Since coming back from being overwhelmed this morning, she'd been holding her feelings together, and didn't want to start panicking... however, she also could not get her feet to move.

When Odin agreed to help a little, she was elated that Amy had found a way to move them forward in their search, but now her deck was full of people. One person was bad enough. Unless it was MacLir, he didn't count, but usually, it was hard for her to spend time with people. Even just one person. Remember to smile, hold her hands still, and prepare phrases to say in a conversation. It was all so draining.

She'd finally got to an acceptable level of comfort to spend longer amounts of time with Amy. Her new friend understood her quirks, and Piper felt safe that she wouldn't be judged for them. Especially after Amy's response to her this morning. Although, even Amy was too much in the company of others. She'd only met Odin and the selkie today and had no time to mentally prepare herself for either.

Flutter bumped her shin, then twined around her legs. "Why are you not moving?" she asked.

"I'm stuck," Piper sent. "Do you think you could take this pan out to the bench?" Piper held out the cake pan, only half-joking.

The kitten beat her wings to reach the countertop and used the height to leap onto Piper's shoulder. Her claws pricked Piper's skin through the lightweight dress. "You smell of fear," she commented, her tail fluffing in response to Piper's alarm. "What on the deck is scaring you?"

Piper sighed. "Just people," she told the kitten.

"I don't like people either," agreed Flutter, adding pointedly, "sometimes they step on your tail."

"It was an accident," Piper said aloud, sending it to the cat mentally as well, but the sound of her own voice was enough to unfreeze her. Flutter purred deeply next to her ear, calming her further. She could do this, she told herself. Everyone would be focused on Amy and the scrying dish. So, Piper could blend into the background. No one was expecting a speech from her or anything. She could do this.

She marched out the door and was halfway through the green room before remembering the dish was supposed to have water in it. Chucking to herself at her folly helped weaken the fear too, so she was calmer by the time she'd filled the dish and gently set it on the bench.

Having heard the story of the scrying in Brigit's infirmary, Piper was a little worried for their ship bench. Thankfully, this time Amy only shifted the shallow pan into a window, not its surroundings.

Edging closer, but not too close to any of the people, she saw Lucky. He was stabbing someone through the chest with a powerful spear. It was good to see him well, and Brigit unharmed too. When they started kissing, Piper rolled her eyes, but smiled. As goddess of love, she'd known for a while they'd get together eventually.

They left the yellow-ish bedroom and entered a white hallway. Stark compared to the friendly yellow, but also lush. Thick white carpets and lavish white wallpaper showed the location as the home of someone with money to spare. Across the hall was another room and Lucky crashed into it.

On the other side was MacLir. Forgetting the people around her, Piper eagerly pushed forward for a better view.

The only light in the bedroom shone in through a slight glow behind the curtains. Any furniture that might have once been in the elegant room was gone. Only a slab of rock and a livid MacLir were in the dark room, tethered to each other with thick boat chains. His skin was as red as the wallpaper from rubbing against the chains to get free. The temper flaring in his eyes reminded everyone he was the most powerful of the elementals.

Lucky leaped forward to help, but with only a spear, could not break the heavy steel links holding MacLir at ankle, wrist, chest, and neck. Finally, Lucky gave up fighting the chain and stepped back, sweat visible on his forehead.

"I think we need a key," said Brigit. She'd followed the lines of the chains and now held a giant lock, hidden out of sight under the edge of the curtains.

"I saw a key," said Piper. She wondered why no one else had seen the obvious key. "Can we tell them a key is outside the door? It's hanging on the wall."

Amy considered for a moment, then said, "Hello! Can you hear me?" When no one gave any sign of hearing her, she said, "Nope, I don't think so. One way scrying only apparently."

"We'll find the key and come back for you," Lucky told MacLir. Piper would have found that calming, but MacLir only became more irate. His muscles strained as he fought against the chains again, only to meet the same defeat. He roared in frustration as Lucky and Brigit hurried out. Back in the empty hall, Brigit found the key.

As the three of them emerged from the MacLir's prison into the bright white hallway, an old man reached the top of the stairs. The man saw the three angry gods free from their chains and locks, and shrieked, "Guards!" He rushed into the nearest room, slamming the door behind him. MacLir led the charge, with the others following closely behind. Lucky had damaged the last two doors, but when MacLir smashed into this third door, it burst apart, splinters flying everywhere.

"Don't move another step!" called the man. When the dust cleared, he held a bundled baby with a small gun pointed at its chest.

"You won't hurt that baby," scoffed Lucky. "You need it for your ceremony."

"I don't need him, though," said the man, tilting the gun barrel to point at Robin, still sleeping on the bed.

MacLir's breath was coming in big huffs. His raw red skin showed signs of cracking, and Piper remembered him saying he was powerless when away from the sea. Also, he was physically weakened in general without the meat of Pig each day, the only food that actually nourished him. It appeared that in his rage, he'd channeled all his remaining energy at the door and was now too unsteady to fight.

Lucky stepped forward, and the man shifted the gun closer to Robin, saying, "Not another step. Throw down your spear and back out of the room."

Guards finally arrived, crowding in behind them. Brigit laid a hand on Lucky's arm. "In surrender, we may learn more than by fighting."

Lucky growled, but obeyed. He disappeared with a pop, but reappeared an instant later without the spear. So, arms raised in surrender, they all backed toward the room's broken entrance.

The man tucked away the gun and clutched the baby tighter. With a haughty sniff, he said, "We leave for the ceremony at the dolmen stone in two minutes. Bring these prisoners along. We can't afford to leave them here and have them escape."

He pushed past the guards and captives, focused on rearranging the infant in his arms, so he didn't see when Brigit lunged out of her guard's grasp and touched Robin's foot. The guard slapped her and grappled to get both arms behind her, then they marched all the prisoners out of the room. The view stayed long enough to see Robin's eyes flutter open, then the window went dark.

"What happened to the view?" Odin asked. "It was getting interesting."

"Sorry, I couldn't hold the vision and think. The stone he just mentioned. I overheard that word before."

"When?" Piper asked Amy urgently. "What else did they say?"

"At the meeting Robin wanted me to spy on, that's what they talked about," said Amy. "Someone said they were setting up at The Burren. Planning to do the ceremony under the Doll Men Stone, even though that still doesn't make sense."

"It makes sense to me," said Odin. "Let's go!"

The selkie clapped her hands and said, "Count the selkies in too!"

Ian

"All the troops are in place and we can begin the ritual preparations," the guard told Ian. "Also, I've sent for the baby."

Ian waved the man away and continued pacing in the clan holding they'd confiscated, a community in The Burren directly under an ancient dolmen stone. The perfect place to finally rid the world of the humans who destroyed the Tua De's way of life all those years ago.

This ritual would be his first, as he'd only practiced the spell but never used it. He knew all the steps, and the first was fire. Guards were stacking firewood in a cleared area of the room below a hole in the ceiling of the cave. They were going to get it as hot as possible using two men with fire magic to stoke the flames.

Blood magic was illegal in the faerie mounds these days. Though, now that he was king, he could make the rules. His clan in the other Tua De community had never stopped using it. To bind loyalty, to adopt children, and more. As the substance that is life, blood could be the most powerful liquid on earth.

Today it would be their weapon. When the baby burned in the white hot fire, its blood would link it to the blood lines of every other human. To burn them away from their realm and the Tua De could finally claim the world for their own. Using MacLir's baby would almost certainly kill MacLir too, an unforseen bonus. With MacLir gone, the extensive search for the pig would be over and Ian's followers could stop cycling that annoying pig through various hiding places.

He had followed his father's plan to perfection. Finding the crow goddess to introduce him to the high court, infiltrating the high court, becoming high king, and now killing all the humans. He hoped his father was watching from whatever afterlife he'd ended up in, because his father would finally see Ian was a better ruler than Tamlin could ever be.

His father's generals would never need to delve into all those extra backup plans Father had written. The books of his father's ramblings that Tamlin religiously studied like a fool. Nope. He would succeed with Plan A and become High King. The victory was only hours away now.

An archaic Tua De crashed through the doors on the far end of the room. "My king! Dire news!" he cried while clutching the baby and waving a gun. Several guards trailed after him. "The prisoners have escaped."

Ian groaned. Why couldn't this last step go smoothly? They could do nothing now and it was better to finish the spell than start over capturing the only people who could stop him. He turned to the guards making the fire. "Faster! Hurry! We'll speed up our plans. We're going to have company soon."

CHAPTER 21

Amy

The heady success of getting Odin to join them after all flowed through Amy. Not only that, but Robin was alive and in better shape than any of the others. The ship flew through the pristine air of the Otherworld toward the western coast of Ireland. Amy marveled again at the beauty of the intact wildness rushing by below them.

Dragging her eyes away from the scenery, she sat cross-legged on the deck and used the scrying pan to watch Robin again. She'd been doing this every few minutes since they left Sweden. He was always running. Closely following the group in front of him until they reached a travel tunnel, then sprang into action, shouting as a distraction to the guards and taking a swing at one. The captives joined the battle in an instant.

Watching anxiously, worried for Robin's safety, Amy watched the three guards around Brigit bonelessly drop to the ground, asleep. MacLir punched out the two closest to him. Lucky kicked in the knees of the one near him, but the guard stumbled to the tunnel portal with the remaining guards as they all disappeared through it.

"Good, they're free," said Odin from behind Amy. "I know that tunnel." Swiftly Odin disappeared with a pop and reappeared in the bowl's image next to Lucky.

"Piper, come look!" Amy called as Odin and Lucky clasped forearms and participated in a manly hug. Piper parked the ship and joined her. Together they watched Odin explain that the girls were on their way, and the selkies were spreading the message to come help.

"I know you are listening," Odin called to the empty air. "I'm not coming back to the ship. I've done my small part to reunite you, and I'm headed home. So, meet in MacLir's throne room. Quick as you can."

"MacLir has a throne room?" Amy asked.

Piper laughed, but nodded. Soon she landed the ship near a big sea cave, and they hurried inside to discover they'd arrived at the same time as the others, coming down opposite hallways.

Saltwater raced into the cave with Piper. Rivulets of ocean traveled through the tunnel next to Piper's bare feet and burst upward to splash the pair in a cold spray of affection as MacLir swept Piper up in his arms. He twirled her, the water swirling around them, healing his cracked skin, then he crushed her with a hug. Neither of them needed to speak to show their joy.

Robin had trailed behind the others, and when he finally reached Amy, he held her close. Sadness infused their hug. His forehead resting on her shoulder, he said, "I'm sorry. I was not strong enough to protect Emily, it's all my fault. I'm so sorry."

Amy stroked his hair. "It's okay, it's okay," she assured him.

"It's not okay, but I swear it will be. It's my fault she's gone and I'll get Emily back."

She didn't know the whole story, but was sure Robin had told the others what happened and Amy would get the rest of the story later. For now, Amy was glad Robin was safe, and they were back together. She kissed him gently and took his hand to follow the others into the wide entrance.

Massive tapestries of underwater landscapes lined the walls, from floor to ceiling in two half-circles, stopping only for the front door and a blue door at the far end of the room. Radiating from a wooden throne, a round blue-green rug left only a small strip of hard-packed earth between the rug and tapestries. Several holes in the ceiling let in shafts of sunlight, dust motes sparkling in the bright afternoon rays shining into the room.

MacLir went through the blue door, but when Piper and Lucky waited by the throne, Amy lingered near the entrance, watching the tunnels. She wondered if they had been followed and didn't want anyone sneaking up on them.

"When MacLir told me he had a room in the mounds," Piper told Amy, "I was shocked when we stayed the night once and he brought me here."

Lucky nodded, understanding her reaction to the odd room. "When the Tuatha De still ruled Ireland, Manannán MacLir was their god. He did not play an active role in our lives, well, except mine, but he was around, the silly trickster. When he became their salvation, they built this suite for him to stay when he visits, a place to settle disputes or meet with people."

"Where are the people he meets supposed to sit?" Amy asked.

"As their new hero, I imagine they didn't think anyone should be sitting in his presence," put in Robin, adding pointedly, "Maybe if he'd been more active in the mounds, their awe of him would not have faded."

MacLir came back in soft brown pants with lighter colored cord laces up the sides. He also wore a large sword on a leather belt and a smaller sword attached to a matching strip of leather slung across his bare chest. "Robin is right. They did not sit around me at first, but they quickly learned I was more casual than all this." MacLir waved vaguely at the brightly colored ocean-creature-themed scenes and the lonely throne. "I never pretended otherwise. I didn't ask for their awe."

He handed a sword to Robin and pointed to Lucky. "Go get the spear."

"But—" Lucky began to protest, then faltered when MacLir cut his eyes to him with a sigh. Lucky flashed away without another word.

"What do I get?" Amy asked.

"You have all the power you need," said MacLir. "Believe in yourself." Lucky popped back with his deadly spear, and MacLir added, "It's time to go."

"Hey, what about me?" Piper asked.

MacLir stroked her cheek and kissed her forehead. "I don't want you in the fighting, but do you remember our visit to the Giant's Playground? I need you to take the ship there and wait for us above ground."

"That's busywork."

"It might not be, depending on who gets hurt and who we find." MacLir kissed Piper goodbye and watched for a moment as she picked her way through the rocks back toward Wave Sweeper. Puddles of seawater streamed around her feet.

MacLir shook himself and led his small resistance to the dirt wall tunnel to begin their sliding and falling journey across the land. Hopefully, to a place where all their enemies were gathering.

On arrival to the mound community closest to The Burren, they were stopped by two guards at the door who peered nervously at each other, but held their ground.

"I need to speak with Ian immediately. Please go tell him I am here," said Lucky.

"Orders are to let no one inside, even us," replied the guards.

As the arguing continued, Amy glanced around the entryway. It was smallish with a low ceiling. It contained the same diffuse light common in the mounds. The room was getting crowded as groups of people dropped out of the solid wall onto the floor in front of the door. Mostly selkies, or so she assumed because they were naked, but also creatures of all shapes and sizes, some armed and others curious about the commotion.

Robin smiled and said, "Do you want to hear something funny? Back when all the legends were happening, a long time ago, there was a minor goddess, I don't remember her name, but she stopped a war on her own."

"Interesting, but how is it funny?"

"She gave every man of the opposing army labor pains!"

Amy laughed, and the beings near them glanced at her inquiringly.

I was thinking," Robin continued, "if everything goes wrong, and you find yourself fighting, maybe you could use that to—."

"Enough!" MacLir shouted from across the room. "Open the door now! Or it will mean your life!"

The guards nodded to each other, and one knocked a complicated code on the door. A second later, the doors burst open. A flood of soldiers waving swords swarmed into the tiny entryway and attacked.

All those who came only to see what was happening jumped back through the wall to leave. The rest stayed to help. Most of the fighters Amy watched were well-matched. Robin was holding his own, and Lucky was clearly holding back. MacLir, with his double swords, was moving too fast to see, wounding men or using the pommel of his big sword to knock them out.

In the world Amy grew up in, swords were a relic of the past, something only seen in movies and museums. In this civilized age, she knew she would never have to worry about a sword wound. This firm internal belief created an invisible bubble of hard air around her, so any sword getting too close bounced off her bubble.

She was grateful for the protection, but this fight was a waste of time. None of these soldiers were important, and no one was getting death blows. In fact, it was like a diversion. A sense of urgency flooded through Amy, reminding her of the waves of labor pains and Robin's story, and she realized what he'd been trying to tell her. If the minor goddess had done it before, it could be done again, right?

Grateful to have no first-hand knowledge of actual birthing, she latched onto the memory of the waves of crushing sample labor pain from her monthly period. Every solider in the entryway fell to the floor, screaming and writhing in pain.

Robin laughed and said, "Unless my guess is wrong, Amy is letting these men experience the joy of childbirth!" He was only partly right, but Amy didn't correct him as Lucky shuddered and led the charge through the now unguarded doors.

As a group, they barged through the double doors into a circular room easily three times as large as MacLir's throne cave. Furniture was pushed to the walls to make space for a massive fire pit. The only two people in the room were Ian and the newborn he held over the fire. .

MacLir strode forward exactly opposite Ian across the wide pit filled with licking tongues of fire, burning in all its colors. Orange, red, blue, and in some places, magically superheated white flames. He shouted over the roaring fire and screaming baby. "Ian! I understand why you have committed the crime of stealing a baby. I know you are angry, but I can explain everything if you pause a moment and listen."

"You are not a leader over me!" Ian cried out, his lips twisted in fury. "We with the pure blood are tired of hiding underground! We want to live under the sun!"

"Nothing is stopping you except your own High Court. You can live anywhere in the human world that you want."

This aggravated the already irate man. "We don't want to live among filthy humans! With the sacrifice of this human baby, I will destroy all the humans, and we, the pure blooded Tuatha Dé Danann, can rule Ireland again. I can be king forever!" Ian began to mutter again, as he had been doing when they came in.

Robin had inched closer as MacLir talked, until he was behind the sea god. He nervously shifted from foot to foot, but his eyes never left Emily.

Ian's voice began to rise, and when MacLir stomped toward him, he said a final word and flipped the baby into the air over the fire. Time slowed as Amy watched MacLir's jaw drop and saw Emily fall, but Robin was ready.

In anticipation of what might happen, he'd braced as close to the fire pit as possible. As soon as Ian let go of the baby, Robin flung his arms out, rigid fingers outstretched. His meager power for moving small objects slowed the baby, and Emily started moving toward Robin, away from her downward trajectory—but not fast enough.

When he realized his power was not strong enough to fight gravity, Robin jumped to catch her. He took a running leap at the deep fire pit and caught Emily in midair, tucking her in his arm like a football. It was a valiant attempt, but also instantly clear he was not going to reach the other side unharmed.

Amy froze, watching the scene in horror. She could not believe she would watch Robin die in a fire. So, he didn't.

Right before he hit the flames, the entire fire pit disappeared, filled in with the usual hard-packed dirt flooring of the faerie mounds. Robin landed hard on his shoulder, still protecting the baby.

Glaring at the man who had caused all this trouble, Amy wondered if lightning sparks really could fly from a person's eyes. A bright light temporarily blinded her, and after she blinked away the bright spots dancing in her vision, she saw the pile of ashes where Ian had stood.

"Oops," Amy said, cringing to see MacLir's grim smile.

"It's okay this time, Amy. But try to improve your control in the future."

CHAPTER 22

Lucky

A headache was coming on. Lucky had overextended his powers today, but it was worth it to help MacLir clean up the mess left by Ian. He drew in more power, and ignored the increased pounding in his brain to hypnotize another prisoner for the next interrogation.

At first, they hoped to find out that most of Ian's followers had been coerced. Now they just wanted to find out who was really in charge. So far, the most common answer to his questions was, "It's time for a final battle with the humans." The man currently in front of them would only reply with the line he'd heard several times from Ian, "We'll be even stronger without humans."

Sitting on his throne a few feet away, MacLir waved his hands, saying, "Stop, stop, enough. I don't want to hear that phrase ever again."

"We are changing our future!" said the hypnotized man earnestly.

"Or that one," snapped MacLir.

The glow in Lucky's eyes faded as he ushered the confused man out of MacLir's aquatic-decorated office into the arms of guards they trusted. One of the guards offered the next imprisoned solider, and Lucky shook his head. "Take them all back to the cells until we figure out what to do with them."

Returning to the center of the room when everyone else was gone, Lucky collapsed onto the floor next to the throne, and MacLir joined him. Stretching out on the plush dusty rug, they both sighed.

"Now what?" asked Lucky.

"Can't your people handle it?"

"You and I talked to the High Court first, and they were the worst of the lot," Lucky reminded MacLir. "You know we can't put them back in power."

"I don't want to put anyone in power. Your own people need to choose the next king and court. Ideally, find a few leaders who are not from a murderous cult aiming for human destruction. Either that, or do without a leader."

"So, you think it's a cult?" asked Lucky.

He wanted MacLir to disagree, to say, of course not. Instead, his mentor sighed again. "This is different than last time." The solemn tone made Lucky glance over. He'd come to accept how MacLir's mind alternated between a wise man and a happy-go-lucky youth. Today MacLir's worried eyes held the weight of years. Centuries trying to keep everyone safe and at peace.

"It's what I was thinking, too," Lucky agreed. "Last time they were fanatical, but hints of new cult ideology were mixed into the political propaganda everyone gave us today. Where would these new opinions have come from?"

"I've never heard any of this before. I'm certain of it. Somehow, I don't think this is over." MacLir hesitated, then propped his head on his elbow to see Lucky. "I need to apologize for not telling you what happened to your father. Cian does have reason to hate me. My idea was to ban him and his followers during the last uprising. They probably only clung to the fact they were banned, instead of understanding it was that or the death the High Court was pushing for."

Lucky would have been astonished to hear this a few weeks ago. However, after his chats with Ian, it was simply another piece of the puzzle.

"My father was a big part of the Voiceless Pure last time, right?"

"Right."

"Yet, he still had children with a human?" asked Lucky. A pointless question. He knew he was the product of one of those unions.

"Many," said MacLir on a sigh. "It was only as part of the war. You were useful to them. A tool for wielding."

Lucky nodded. It all explained so much. Even truths he'd known, but didn't want to examine too closely. Like his father feeding Ian lies about their birth while knowing both his half-magic children would die in the ritual he'd prepared. "Maybe the cult didn't start here. Could it be spreading from another colony? One where my father lived?"

MacLir flattened onto his back again, his head resting on his hands. "We banned your father. Along with his thirty or so followers and their wives, some of the most powerful Tua De, they would have been weakened away from Ireland. It's been assumed they are dead since they've never been heard from since."

"Ian had to come from somewhere. He claimed to live in a colony with my father and that someone was bringing them pieces of Pig to maintain his immortality."

"A worrying thought. It implies allies here who knew they were alive and were willing to break the rules for them. Presumably, some of the older High Court members, as their belief in The Voiceless Pure was the strongest. They must have hidden it all these years. Which brings us back to our original problem. Choosing new leaders will be difficult. And I refuse any involvement this time."

"I'll talk to Brigit and see what can be done," promised Lucky.

As they both lapsed into a comfortable silence, Lucky's thoughts wandered to Brigit and he decided to go see her about his headache. He glanced over at MacLir to tell him he was headed out and realized the boy had fallen asleep. Leaving the sea god on the ground to rest, he made his way to the infirmary. His head was doing better, so Brigit would see through the excuse to visit, but maybe she wouldn't mind.

In fact, he was beginning to realize there was a lot she wouldn't mind doing with him beyond healing a mostly gone headache. Dreams of a home together flitted through his mind, but where? Not underground, obviously. The living conditions were appalling.

The realization almost stopped him in his tracks. If he didn't want to live or raise children here, why would any of his people want to? He internally smiled at his thought of children, but resolved to seriously consider how to help the overcrowded living situation in the faerie mounds.

He'd made it to her hallway and had his hand on the doorknob when someone rushed up from behind him and ruffled his hair. He flipped around with an angry remark ready. "How dare—"

"I knew I'd find you here," said MacLir, his lips twisting in a smirk, his eyebrows raised with a glance at Brigit's door. "One of the guards came back with a prisoner we didn't talk to. This man says he was coerced, and now it's starting to wear off. He didn't want to help them, but he had access to some items they needed, so his memories were suppressed. The memories are returning, but more importantly, he knows where Pig is being kept and told me where to find him."

"Do you trust him?"

"Maybe, but we don't have any other leads. Let's go."

Amy

"It's a terrible idea," said Piper, her fingers fluttering as she found the words to say. "How can you trust this man? This anonymous tip?"

"I have nowhere else to look."

"To look," repeated Piper thoughtfully. "Yes, actually. What if we could look?"

"I've been looking!" MacLir plopped on the bench, but Piper's gaze had turned to Amy.

Amy had been watching the pair argue it out for several minutes, staying out of it like Lucky while standing near the ladder, but that wouldn't be an option based on the gleam in Piper's eyes. "Amy, you can scry to see if it's a trap."

"Well… I'm happy to try, but, what am I supposed to see?"

"The pig," Lucky stage-whispered to her.

Amy laughed. "I know what you need to find, but I've never met this pig. I've only ever scryed for people I've seen before." Her mind turned to people she'd scryed last time, like Robin or Maclir, even the selkie she'd met. Trying new magic was fine, but how to tell her magic what to search for? "Do you have a picture or something I can use as a focus?"

A photo and a dish of water were quickly provided as MacLir transitioned the ship and everyone on it into the Otherworld. The window Amy made showed the outside of a little country corner store. A man slouched out front, a small light showing his lit cigarette in the dark. An old woman at the counter was visible through the bright shop window.

"I know that shop," exclaimed Piper. "It's in the village next to the main mounds. We've been there together before."

"It's where the man said the Pig is. See, everything's fine," said MacLir.

As it happened with the selkie, the focus of vision zoomed in. Through the store, through the wooden planks of the floor, and into a semi-dark cellar. In one corner, next to big boxes of cans, Pig was tethered to a heavy metal shelf by a rope around his neck. He didn't appear worried or harmed. Amy breathed a sigh of relief for MacLir, and the window went blank. "Oh, sorry, I should have held that longer."

"No, it's fine. Now we know exactly where to go."

Oddly, when they arrived, the same man was still outside the store, cigarette smoke drifting into the dusky sky, and he tipped his old-fashioned flat cap at them. Amy was so lost in thought that she was last to troop through the door and walked into a bizarre scene.

The rug was pushed back from the trapdoor, but two men ran up the steps with knives. The old woman behind the counter was shouting, "Now, now!".

MacLir dodged the first knife-wielder, pushing Piper behind him, almost crushing her between his back and rack of wine. As bottles crashed and broke around her feet, Piper tensed and shut her eyes tight, something Amy recognized as trying to block out the overwhelming noise.

Wondering if she should help or get out of the way, she remembered the man outside. Amy started toward the door to ask the man for help, but he was already crouching in the doorway. His hands were on the wooden floor, causing the planks to buckle. The motion spread outward and knocked Lucky off his feet.

Glancing around for a weapon, she found a heavy vase filled with flowers and bashed it solidly against the man's head. When he fell sideways, the old woman rushed around the counter waving a short sword.

Without her stronger Otherworld power and no other handy weapons, Amy backed away and shouted for help.

The cramped store gave her nowhere to run and she didn't know any self-defense moves against a sword. The woman advanced quickly, and Amy crossed her arms in front of her head to ward off the blow that would hit any moment, ready to at least kick the woman in the knees.

When the attack didn't come, Amy peeked between her arms in time to finish watching the woman slip in the water from the vase. The old woman fell next to the downed man, but her head hit the counter first, and she lay still.

Adrenaline still pounding in her ears, she rushed over to the basement door to help and discovered both knives had been removed from their owners. Piper was unharmed, but muttering, "A trap. Another trap."

Amy wished she could give her a reassuring pat. Instead, she pointed to Piper's pocket and rubbed her fingers together. Taking the hint with a grateful smile, Piper pulled out her worry stone and flipped it between her fingers, causing her shoulders to visibly relax.

After briefly examining the rest of the store for anyone hiding, Lucky and MacLir disappeared into the basement.

MacLir returned first, helping a young man navigate the steps. Little more than a teen, he had red marks around his mouth and hands. His uniform, with a logo matching the store's sign, appeared stained and shabby as if it had been lived in for days.

Next, Lucky appeared, leading a gigantic black and white spotted pig. At the top, the pig's rough rope was removed with a loving scratch and pat from Lucky. The hefty animal trotted toward Piper and MacLir in excitement when he found himself free, his belly swinging and hoofs clacking. He ambled from friend to friend to accept their affection, as they petted his ears and scratched his chin, assuring Pig of his braveness as he radiated his happy mood to the group.

CHAPTER 23

Lucky

The fluffy gray kitty flitted from person to person, gathering love, masterfully avoiding the string lights and bunting hanging above the small group of friends. Friends who were becoming almost like a family. Flutter picked her way around the table to Lucky and rolled onto her back, exposing her belly, patiently waiting for a tummy rub.

Lucky gingerly tickled her chin and tummy until she attacked his hand. Then she jumped up and fluttered away to someone else. On his right sat Brigit, tapping her foot to the music and daintily eating a lemon bar.

MacLir and Piper sat beyond her, fooling around with their food like toddlers. Trying to feed each other a variety of desserts, they'd managed to make a mess on both their faces. MacLir scooted his dining chair forward and licked cream directly off Piper's cheek. She squealed while laughing and playfully batted him away.

Clara sat alone at the head of the table, but instead of being lonely, she was smiling at the antics of the younger generation. He knew that smile. Happy in the moment, happy watching the younger generation, but definitely life-weary–his community's term for the people who lived long and whose minds gave out even when their bodies persisted. He didn't know humans could become life-weary.

He remembered thinking it might be happening to him. Actually, the day he'd met Piper. But now? No. Everything had changed.

"You want the last bite?" Brigit asked, offering the last bite of lemon curd on shortbread.

Inspired by MacLir's shenanigans, he nodded and opened his mouth, a grin crinkling his eyes. Brigit giggled. He could see the younger Brigit in that laugh. She hesitantly reached out and dropped the tidbit into his open mouth with another laugh.

Their hosts were smiling, but appeared calm and collected. Watching from across the table, all traces of coercion gone from his mind, Robin had his arm around Amy's shoulders and she leaned into him. Lucky thought again about how Robin's devotion to righting the wrong that was not his fault had put him directly in danger. It was… touching. Perhaps the boy was growing on him.

A night of laughter and chatting made him realize he had been more lonely than he'd wanted to admit. No more, though. Now, he was included in this group of found family, formed by Piper and MacLir. His life, as ever, was enriched by the welcome meddling of MacLir.

When the dinner party finally broke up, he assisted Brigit in rising. "Can I walk you home?" he asked. She nodded, her hand still in his. He caught and held her eyes, then kissed her palm. The usually confident woman's eyelashes fluttered, and she gave him a shy smile.

At the door, everyone kissed cheeks and hugged except for Piper and Clara, who stood together several steps away but smiled and waved at people. With many "Let's do this again soon," and "See you next week," and "Thanks for a lovely evening," everyone finally departed for their homes.

Lucky and Brigit ambled the Dublin streets in companionable silence, slipping into the garden and strolling hand in hand along the paths under the moonlit night. Brigit's closeness overwhelmed Lucky, as ever. Even away from her medicines all day, the scent of herbs and plants still wafted around her willowy form.

Her green eyes flashed at him as they caught the light, and he could no longer resist. Pulling her even closer, crushing her against him, he captured her lips in his. She gladly joined him. When Lucky was too light-headed to stand, they collapsed onto a bench and paused for breath. He kept Brigit close, and she laid her head on his shoulder. He wondered if she could hear how his heart was racing with the joy of holding her near.

"I don't want to bury any more children," Brigit said. Lucky's mind struggled with the meaning of the words and her tone of voice. What could this sentence have to do with their shared passion moments ago? Before he could ask, she continued, "This modern world is both more secure and less, but with MacLir's help, children have every chance of lasting longer than myself this time."

Her words sounded hopeful. Nearly coy. Her tone matched the previous mood, but he was still unpacking her words, trying to force them into the context of the situation.

"Do you remember when Amy pulled me aside earlier tonight? She confessed something to me."

"Oh, really?" Lucky said, his reply on autopilot while his mind raced. Why was she having a casual conversation after a kiss so long it took his breath away?

"She accidentally made me fertile." Brigit tilted her head to meet his eyes and grinned. Squeezing his hand where their fingers were still laced together.

"Oh?" he said, then what she said sunk in along with the twinkle in her eye. "Oh!"

"Yes. She says we're having a boy."

Trying to take in all the implications of this statement, Lucky's blood rushed in his ears. He wanted to dance with joy and cry with happiness. Still speechless, he pulled Brigit to him, burying his face in her hair, and she molded willingly into him. They had a future. Together.

When they eventually traveled through the portal, they arrived to see the mounds in chaos. Screams and shouts echoed through the tunnels, and the ground was littered with pamphlets. Lucky picked one up. The headline read, "If Ian is dead, it's because he was murdered for his ideals!" Below this startling statement was a paragraph that gave Lucky chills. A message to his followers that now was the time to rise up. Time to act. It was signed by The Voiceless Pure.

Piper

Leaving a party was actually something sad for once. The social dinner was surprisingly fun. After dreading going all week, she'd had a wonderful time. With only people she knew and who knew her well, she'd relaxed into a person she'd never known she could be around so many people.

With a start, she realized it was similar to spending time around her aunt's family. Her aunt, her aunt's husband, and their kids. They had all made her feel welcome and wanted. From MacLir and her unusual comfort around him, to her eventual comfort around Amy and Lucky, and the people they loved. Even Clara was not someone to hide her true self around. Clara understood.

Her sense of them was similar to what she felt with her aunt. Like family. Each and every one of them. A warmth started in her chest, flowing to the tips of her fingers and toes. She'd done what she set out to do and more.

"You are quiet tonight." MacLir swung Emily inside a basket with one arm and swung her hand in his other as they arrived at the empty field where Wave Sweeper waited for them in the Otherworld.

Piper rubbed his hand with a thumb to show him she heard his words.

"So, I saw you reading Lucky's future," he began.

"How could you know?"

MacLir steadied her on the ladder, and their conversation paused as they got onboard. Flutter launched from Piper's shoulder and slipped into the cabin. The kitten's tail swished as it disappeared into the inky darkness of the hallway. Moonlight bathed the deck in an ethereal glow, so much stronger in the Otherworld realm, where the air was sweet and clean.

Sitting on the bench, MacLir gently placed Emily's basket on the deck and patted the spot next to him. Piper sat, but tucked her legs onto the bench and rolled toward him, so her head was in his lap. He stroked her hair as he continued their conversation. "I could tell you read Lucky's future as we said goodbye. It's a blank stare you get… and he was the one you stared at."

"You are right. But he didn't need my help."

"Do you ever read my future?"

Piper hesitated. She didn't know why he asked, but gave him a truthful answer. "No. It's intruding on your privacy."

He shook with a laugh that almost knocked her off the bench. "So, you are fine intruding on other people's privacy?"

"Sure, it's for a good cause. Their future happiness."

"What about our future happiness? Look into my future."

Piper focused, staring into MacLir's unnaturally aqua blue eyes. A color she'd never seen on a human. His hair was completely dry for once, still spiked out in odd directions, stiff from seawater. She shut her eyes as the mental pictures approached, ready to wash over her.

She saw their first meeting. Him springing out of the ocean. Her shouting, "You splashed the ocean on me." What she'd missed at the time was how he examined her, and how interested he seemed. The saltwater misting in the air and catching the light faded as she heard the final words of the vision.

"I'm MacLir."

"I'm Piper."

"I know."

Transitioning to the second vision of the two of them in love, she was caught off guard by watching herself from a moment ago. Cuddled on the small bench, her head in his lap, his arms encircled her so she didn't fall off. MacLir saying, "What about our future happiness? Look into my future."

Finally, the third vision appeared. A snippet of their future happiness. A toddler ran toward them from calm ocean waves. Sand clinging to her chubby feet, her bouncing golden curls and aqua eyes reminded Piper of MacLir. The girl launched herself in Piper's arms, and MacLir surrounded them both with a hug.

When the final vision faded, the level of urgency required to get to that future moment was powerful. In couples already together, she never sensed any urgency, but in this vision, the urgency was the strongest she'd experienced.

"So, what did you see?" asked MacLir, adding tiny random braids to her long hair as he waited for her to speak.

"I've already met the man I could fall in love with." Piper smiled softly up at MacLir. "And we found a way to create a baby that was a blend of us both. We have the potential to live happily ever after… but it felt like multiple steps still stand between us and a future with all of us together.”

A worried frown line creased MacLir's forehead, and as Piper brushed it away she remembered the chat she had with Amy earlier, about her concerns for the future during a quiet moment before the party. After explaining the vague sense Piper was getting about her future, Amy had replied, “If you are worried it won't happen it's because you don't want it badly enough to make it happen for yourself. You have to believe.”

“That's not how life works,” Piper blurted out, but then, was not sure that statement was true.

“Of course it is,” said Amy with a shrug.

Piper thought about how bad she wanted a baby and how it had happened. Maybe Amy was right. Was believing in herself all it took to mold the life she desperately wanted?

Amy

Plates clinked, and silverware rattled as Amy slid everything into a sink of soapy water. The dinner party was a success. Something she had carefully planned for. From the low lighting and non-repetitive quiet music to the structured schedule and enforced end time. She planned every detail with the comfort of Piper and Clara in mind, and it worked. They'd both had a great time.

Amy washed and handed everything piece by piece to Clara to rinse and stack in a draining rack.

“You were gone so long, yet you look the same,” said Clara, finally sharing what Amy knew had been bothering her.

All those days searching for the captives she'd been pulled in and out of the parallel realm. It had seemed fine in the moment, but now the time difference between realms was painfully clear. Her sister's teens were adults and Clara was much older. Her once lithe shape, ruined after birthing children, was now even more pear-shaped. Laugh lines and sagging skin showed the passage of time, although Clara's eyes still held a playful gleam and her hair was still as wildly curly. "I was in the Otherworld to find Robin, and time is so different there," Amy replied with a shrug.

"I know," sighed Clara, "I'm still trying to wrap my head around it. I really missed you."

Amy nodded, not trusting herself to speak without crying for their lost time together. Changing the subject, she asked, "Do you think I should stay here with Robin? At least, for a while?"

"Do you love him?" Clara asked.

After all these months living with Robin, she was more attached to him than when this all started. MacLir had offered Amy immortality, to stay with Robin, and Brigit had explained it was a daily renewal, so she could stop anytime and return to being mortal, yet, she hesitated in accepting the offer. Robin said he understood and would support either choice, to stay mortal or stay with him, and she felt that he meant it.

"Your lack of answer is telling. If you don't want to stay here, then live with me," Clara said. "Come with me on my flight home tomorrow. You don't have to go back to your old room—I know how you feel about mom—so you can sleep in my guest bedroom until you start college."

It was a kind offer, but not a tempting one. Amy collected her thoughts to reply, and Clara pushed on in a serious tone, rare for her. "Don't stay with a man you don't love. I did it, and I'm not happy. So don't do what I did."

Her cheerful sister rarely complained, but Amy knew Clara was unhappy with the man who made her life difficult. Robin was different, though. Amy could not imagine him doing any of the irritating actions Clara's husband did every day. Maybe she had not lived with Robin long enough. Or, perhaps she was in love and blind to his annoying habits—for now.

Or, what if she became a problem to him? Robin had patience with her outbursts of temper this year, but what about next year? And the years after that? More than his patience, he showed love in other little ways through their days together. He was clearly in love, but was she? Quietly, as if testing the words, Amy said, "Maybe… I am in love?"

Clara smiled. Her whole body wiggled in a strange happy dance, making her wild hair bounce. All seriousness gone from her tone, she replied, "Oooo, yay for a chance at love and happiness, so if you are unsure, I think you should stay here and go for it. Besides, you're not staying here for long right? You and Robin are going galavanting across the world. Didn't I hear Robin say you two are headed to Egypt next week?"

"Well, he's already seen some of Europe, so he thought it would be fun if we went somewhere new to both of us, at least for our first adventure."

"Watch out for camels. They spit," said Clara, splashing Amy with sink water.

Amy snapped a towel at her in return, but her imagination was painting pictures of desert sunsets and writing stories in the shadow of the sphinx.

"You'll have lots of time to see the world now that you are immortal to stay with Robin, right? I'll be gone in a blink for you," said Clara wistfully. "You'll have to remember me fondly as that crabby old crone back in the mists of time. My part in raising you will be part of your origin story. The horse-riding wild witch of the southwest who prepared a goddess for the world."

Trying to disperse Clara's somber mood, Amy said, "You're never crabby." Then she made a face she knew would cause Clara to laugh.

Clara giggled so hard she snorted, switching the somber mood to Amy, who knew she'd miss her sister too much. She didn't mind not seeing the rest of her family, but was worried Clara was right about being gone soon compared to Amy's new lifespan. She hoped her sister could move closer to her new home in Ireland, so they could spend as much time together as possible. Everything would be perfect if all the people she loved lived in one place.

Tonight was perfect though. The couples around the dinner table, Piper's new baby, and travel plans with Robin. "It's a lovely happy ending," said Amy.

Clara watched the water cascading over her hands and the dinner plate she held. "Yes. For the moment. But happy endings are fleeting, temporary events... because life keeps moving on."

If you enjoyed this book please leave a review and share with friends!

Follow the author on your favorite platform to find out about upcoming books.

Read More in:

Treasure in the Deep
Wave Sweeper Trilogy Book 3

Read the exciting conclusion of Piper's adventures in Wave Sweeper Trilogy's Book 3, *Treasure in the Deep,* where Piper finds a way to make her powers stronger, and the real threat to the faerie mounds finally becomes clear enough to fight, if MacLir and Lucky and all their friends have the combined strength to win.

BIO

Starr Green is an autistic author living in the Pacific Northwest and has a degree specializing in Environmental Communication from Oregon State University. As a teen, she was delighted by all the worlds she discovered in the local library. Her debut novel Castaway Strangers was the first of her many fantasy books with female autistic characters.

Find out more at: earthyinfo.wordpress.com

Books by Starr Green:

•

CASTAWAY STRANGERS

•

Wave Sweeper Trilogy
SAILING IN THE SKY
BELIEF IN THE REALM
TREASURE IN THE DEEP *(Coming Soon)*

•

www.ingramcontent.com/pod-product-compliance
Lightning Source LLC
Chambersburg PA
CBHW031015190726
48286CB00003BA/855